I0591555

THE WRITE HOUSE

A NOVELLA

STUART FABE

The Write House
A Novella
Copyright 2022 by Stuart Fabe

All Rights Reserved

No part of this publication can be reproduced, stored in a retrieval system, or transmitted, in any form or by any means — electronic, mechanical, photo-reproductive, recording, or otherwise — without prior written permission by the publisher, except for the inclusion of brief quotations in a review.

For more information about this title or to order books, contact the publisher:

    Stuart A. Fabe
    Greencastle, Indiana
    stuartfabe@gmail.com

ISBN: 978-0-578-29211-3 (softcover)
           979-8-218-00169-8 (eBook)

Printed in the United States

Cover photo by Stuart Fabe

Author's Note

"Language is the currency of thought."

"Plots are the vehicles on which stories ride.
Characters are their pilots and passengers."

I am a person of my times.
I was born in the middle of the fifth month
in the last year of the first half
of the twentieth century.
May 14, 1949.
Someday I will cease to exist as a sentient
life-form, but until that day I will remain
eternally grateful to whatever spirit
imbued me with a creative yearning.

Stuart Fabe
Greencastle, Indiana
2022

Dedication

For Carol and LaWayne Engelstad

Inspirational Friends
Whose Home Is a Tribute to Imagination.

Chapter 1

Putnam County, Indiana

1920

Delano Engel and his lovely wife, Caroline, casually walk along a path atop the rim of the limestone quarry a few miles west of Greencastle, Indiana. It's a stunning bluebird day with the late April sun finally providing some warmth to their world after a harsh midwestern winter. Hand in hand, they walk slowly just happy to be together after Delano's harrowing combat tour of France in World War I. He's only been back home for a few months, after having served abroad under the command of General "Black Jack" Pershing for nearly two years. When he returned he was a changed man. He's no longer just the naive, rosy-cheeked young fella Caroline had bid adieu to at the train station like so many other couples and families.

No, at age twenty-two Delano Engel had witnessed the world that he thought he knew morph into a living hell in the trenches and came to understand the ugly meaning of the phrase "no man's land." The sights of dismembered bodies, the screams and sobs that never seemed to end, the cordite smells from artillery fire, and the gagging odor of rotting corpses and human waste. Then, there was the constant fear of noxious chemicals that wafted on the wind.

Yet, Delano Engel did what millions of other soldiers didn't do. He survived. He was bone-weary and shell-shocked both by the never-ending cannon and mortar fire, and his spirit was shocked as well.

Now, back home with Caroline, he's slowly returning to a loving world that he'd nearly forgotten while enduring the horrors of war.

Caroline gently squeezes his hand as they walk along quietly taking in the lush spring greenery and the sounds of birds and squirrels chattering away searching for mates and preparing their nests. She looks at Delano and knows that he's a different man. His eyes are closed and his face bears an expression that tells her that most, but not all of him, has fully returned from the war. There's no doubt in her mind that he still loves her, but she feels sadness for him and frustration about what she can do to help the only man she's ever loved.

"C'mon, Delano, let's sit on this large rock. Remember how we'd come here when you were first trying to figure out how to kiss me?"

Delano smiles at the thought and gives Caroline's hand a gentle squeeze. "Yeah, it's our special rock, huh? I was so awkward back then, but I knew I had to risk kissing you or just burst!"

"Well, sir, there are plenty more kisses where that came from," she promises and leads him over to the huge limestone slab. At first they just sit quietly staring into the quarry below and at the trees surrounding the rim's perimeter providing a verdant balm for the eyes. The warm sun, gentle breeze, and Caroline's presence bring a grateful tear to his eye as he wonders how he was ever so lucky to return home from Europe.

Caroline had promised herself that she wouldn't ask Delano many questions about his wartime experience. She knows it had to have been horrible. If he wants to talk, he'll talk, and she'll listen.

Delano looks at Caroline and strokes her golden hair. He puts his arm around her and draws her closer. They sit like that for a few moments watching the buzzards riding the updrafts high above the quarry, and then Delano speaks softly, "Look at those marvelous creatures, Caroline, soaring as if they don't have a care in the world. That's what I want for us. Freedom from people telling us what to do, freedom to build our own dreams. When I was in France, I promised myself that if I made it back to you, I would do whatever it took for us to be happy. And, when I saw those aerial balloons and airplanes over the trenches, I dreamed that someday we could fly like them...without the bullets, of course."

Caroline leans her head on Delano's shoulder, and whispers, "I have total faith in you, my love."

They get up from the limestone slab and continue walking along the rim of the quarry. Occasionally, chipmunks peek at them from holes and small crevices, and sulphur moths flit about in the warm air looking like flecks of gold floating before them. Before long, they reach the Reflection Center, and Caroline and Delano take a little break for water, and to enjoy the center's magnificent architecture.

"Whoever designed this place sure knew how to blend the building with its natural setting. It's just so peaceful," Caroline offers.

"Yes, peaceful," Delano whispers as they sit again on a teak bench beside a small brook.

Almost simultaneously, they both say, "There's something I need to tell you!" They both laugh at the coincidence and insist that the other go first in sharing their thoughts. Finally, Delano relents and blurts out, "I bought an aeroplane!"

"You what?!" Caroline replies, her eyes as wide as saucers! "You bought a what?!" And then she begins to laugh, thinking that maybe Delano's kidding.

"I bought a Curtiss JN 4." Delano sees that Caroline is understandably bewildered and says, "I know...I should've told you. Better yet, I should've asked your opinion before I agreed to buy it, but well, the opportunity arose, and I leaped at it." Delano winces a little expecting to get a stern, adult response from his practical wife, but instead she curiously says, "Tell me about it...and please tell me we can afford our own aeroplane!"

Delano is over-the-moon with excitement, and Caroline is delighted to see her husband as happy as he is. He responds informatively as if to confirm the practicality of his purchase, "Well, she's a Curtiss JN-4, and she's called a Curtiss Jenny because of the JN designation. She's a biplane and was built by the Curtiss Aeroplane Company in Hammondsport, New York. The Jenny is constructed of wood, mostly spruce, and has a top speed of 75 miles per hour. She was flown as a trainer for airmen, primarily in the U.S. Army Air Service and the England's

Royal Flying Corps. Our Jenny was built in 1918, so she's practically brand new. This JN 4 is actually the fourth model of this aeroplane, and it's already proving to be the backbone of American postwar civil aviation. Darling, planes are the future, and I want us to be part of that future."

"Well, with you describing the plane as a 'she', I guess I'll have another female to contend with, huh? And, please tell me it doesn't have bullet holes in it, does it?!"

"Of course not, silly, they've all been repaired, good as new."

"You're not serious, are you, Delano?!"

"No, of course not. I guess I shouldn't tease you at a moment like this, and yes, we can afford it. My inheritance and our family's business interests have left us in pretty good shape. Since the end of the war, thousands of surplus Jennys have been sold at bargain prices to private owners like us. Recently, I read a newspaper article in which folks are describing this period as the barnstorming era. I suppose I should also tell you that I've been learning to fly her these past two months and have even soloed several flights."

"You what?!" Caroline stammers. And then her eyes sparkle, and she surprises her husband by asking, "What was it like?!"

Delano gets really excited again and says, "It's like nothing I've experienced before. The engine is a little loud, and it can get a bit chilly up there, but darling, flying is the most magnificent sensation in the world, and what one can see from up there is beyond description. And you know what's the best part?" he asks.

"Successfully landing, I hope!" she jests.

"Well, that, too," he agrees, "but the best thing is that it has two cockpits, so we can fly our Jenny together."

Again, Caroline giggles a little nervously, but it's clear to Delano that his wife is game. "So," Delano asks, "what did you want to share with me, darling?"

"Uh, and where do you plan on storing our new aeroplane? You know our little apartment doesn't exactly have proper accommodations for something that big."

"Well, Greencastle has a new airfield with land that Al Stanley sold to Putnam County, and I've rented hangar space for it. In fact, now that I've spilled the beans, do you wanna go check her out? But, you didn't answer my question about what you wanted to share."

Caroline pauses for a moment trying to muster up the right words and suggests, "Well, we might want to look for an aeroplane with three cockpits."

"I don't think they make aeroplanes with three cockpits, darling," and then it dawns on him. "You mean…" Delano blurts in shock.

"Yes, dear, we're going to have a baby, and no, we can't name it Jenny. Apparently, that name has already been taken."

"Well, I guess we better begin house hunting, then. We're definitely going to need more room and a proper yard."

Caroline grabs his hand and pulls him to his feet and laughs out loud, "What makes you think I haven't already started!"

Chapter 2

AFTER WALKING A MILE or so, Caroline and Delano return to their modest apartment, and he tosses her the keys to their Ford Model T. "You drive, Caroline. You might as well get used to being an independent woman because in this day and age the sky's the limit."

"You've got that right!" she returns. "Strap in, Delano, it's going to be a bumpy ride!" And off they go…

Fifteen minutes later Caroline follows Delano's directions, and they arrive at a broad open stretch of land surrounded by acres upon acres of newly planted fields.

"Head over to that large barn," he says. They get out and walk to the rear of the Tin Lizzie and Delano opens the trunk. "Here, let's put these coveralls on, and we'll need these goggles."

Once properly clothed they walk over to the barn and are greeted by the airfield's manager and top mechanic, Brian Helton. "Gonna go up again, Delano?" Brian asks. "Gonna be dark before too long, but you still have a couple of hours of good daylight left. The Jenny's fueled up and ready to go. Is this your first flight, Mrs. Engel?"

"Yes, indeed it is!" she replies. "Anything special I need to know?"

"Naw, just sit tight and enjoy the scenery. Your husband's become a very good pilot in a brief amount of time. It's a little scary at first, but you'll do fine. I hear tell there's a woman named Amelia Earhart who's already a flying legend. Maybe you'll be next!"

Caroline shakes her head doubtfully as she settles into the front cockpit.

A few moments later Delano switches on the magneto and calls down to Brian, "Ready when you are, Mr. Helton."

Brian walks to the aeroplane's propeller and gives it a hefty yank, then another, and the Jenny's engine roars to life. He removes the wooden blocks holding the wheels and helps push the sturdy aircraft out of the hangar. Delano checks the air sock for wind direction and examines the ailerons, cables, and gauges. He gives a thumbs-up sign to Brian and slowly taxis to the field's long grass runway.

"Ready, darling!" he shouts to Caroline. "Here we go!" The biplane lumbers a few yards into takeoff position, and Delano takes a final look around to make sure everything's clear. He pushes the Jenny's throttle forward, and it quickly picks up speed. The wheels lift off from terra firma, and he smiles broadly as he hears Caroline scream, "Woohoooo!"

The late afternoon weather is glorious. The skies are bluebird blue with a few billowing clouds high above. Delano guides the plane upward, then upward more until he arrives at his desired cruising altitude two thousand feet above rolling Putnam County farmland. He looks at Caroline and sees that her knuckles are no longer white and that she's looking all around like a kid on Christmas morning. She hollers something barely audible to Delano, then screams "Woohooo!" again.

Delano banks the Jenny starboard and makes a sweeping arc toward Greencastle and lowers the plane's altitude so they can get a good look at the town's old courthouse and several merchant shops like Prevo's men's haberdashery. Again, Caroline shouts something barely audible over the roar of the engine, and Delano sees her point in a direction she wants him to fly. They cruise over the Andrew Carnegie library and then head toward the Dunbar covered bridge over Big Walnut Creek. Once past the creek Delano guides the Jenny south toward the limestone quarry that they'd visited earlier. Caroline is mesmerized by what she sees and can't believe how tiny everything looks on the ground.

Delano reduces their altitude to about seven hundred feet, and they approach a heavily wooded area that looks totally different to them from the air. "Look there!" Caroline shouts and points to a tiled roof tower jutting up from the trees. She makes a circular motion with her finger, and Delano understands that she wants to look at the tower again. He lowers their altitude to about three hundred feet, and they both spy an old Victorian house that they'd never seen before. Delano makes a few more passes above the mansion to give them a better look, and Caroline looks mesmerized by the old house situated in its secluded location.

Delano taps Caroline on her shoulder, and she looks back and sees him tapping his watch indicating it's time to head back to the airfield. They fly over the courthouse square again and the new library building, then make a couple of passes over Asbury College's campus. Caroline can't help but think that the school's original East College building looks about the same vintage as the old house they'd just seen. A few minutes later the Jenny is circling Putnam County airport's grass runway, and the young aviators see Brian come out of the hangar to greet them. Delano reduces the plane's altitude and speed, and Caroline grips the sides of her cockpit as Delano deftly sets the Curtiss Jenny's wheels on the grass and guides it toward Brian and the hangar.

They get out of the aeroplane, and Delano doesn't even need to ask Caroline what she thought of the flight. The look on her face is one of pure delight. She wraps her husband in a great hug and says, "I see what you meant back at the quarry. I want this to be our future, too, Del!"

———

The next day Caroline is still in awe of the sensation of flying and what they could see from the air. Delano can barely get a word in edgewise by her enthusiasm. "Let's go see if we can find that old house we saw hidden in the trees. Do you think we can find it? Maybe it's for sale."

"Maybe," Delano replies. "I have a general idea where it might be, but I'm not sure if there's easy access to the property with our Model T, but yeah, we can take a look, and we can also scour the county's real estate records for details, if need be."

After breakfast Delano and Caroline work around their apartment doing a few household chores and then get cleaned up.

"Are you ready to go?" Delano shouts out to Caroline. Then he looks outside and sees that she's already in their Model T's driver's seat with the engine running.

"Is somebody excited?!" he teases as he settles into the passenger's seat. I don't know what's got you pumped up more, driving the Model T or flying in Jenny."

"Which way, Mr. Smartypants? We're burning daylight!"

"Head out West Walnut Street toward the quarry. I think I spotted an old carriage lane when we went for our hike yesterday."

Caroline gives the Tin Lizzie some gas and Delano hangs onto his seat. A few minutes later they approach what appears to be a broad grassy path with an old split rail fence running along either side. From the road it doesn't appear that anyone has entered the area for a very long time.

"Pull in here, Caroline, and please go slowly. We don't know how solid the ground is under the grass, and we sure don't want to bust an axle." Caroline does as he asks and in about a hundred yards they see a large grove of mature walnut trees with a wooden post and weathered old sign bearing the name Wright with a metal "no trespassing" sign beneath it.

"What do ya think, Del? Think they're serious about the no trespassing."

"Probably, but it looks like a darn old sign, and I'm willing to risk it if you are. Pull ahead slowly and let's see if anyone's around."

Caroline nods affirmatively and inches the car forward. In about another fifty yards, the grassy pathway veers to the left, and they see a handsome Victorian carriage house painted barn red, and beyond that a magnificent brick mansion that looks as if it's been unoccupied for quite some time. Delano and Caroline smile expectantly at each other and pull up to the house and get out. They quickly glance at the stout brick edifice and nod enthusiastically.

"Hellooo! Anybody home?" Delano calls out. "Hello!" he calls again, but no one replies. "Why don't you check the carriage house, Caroline, and I'll knock on the door."

Delano steps onto the porch and notices that it hasn't been swept for a long time, probably many months gauging from the amount of leaves and twigs that occupy various corners and on the window sills. He knocks on the door and calls out again,

"Hello, anyone home?!" Again, no reply. Delano shades his eyes and presses his nose to the door's window and peers inside. The interior appears empty, and he goes to another window and looks inside. He sees what appears to be an entry hall with fine floors and decorative wooden molding. "This place is amazing," he whispers to himself. He leaves the porch and walks around the perimeter of the house, thinking that the owners may be working in the yard, but he sees no one.

"There you are," Caroline says breathlessly as she joins him.

"What did you see at the carriage house? Anything that indicates that the house is occupied?"

"No. The door was locked, but I managed to peek inside, and it's empty, like no one has used it for quite a while."

"Yeah," Delano confirms. "I peered inside a couple of windows and saw no sign of life either. One thing's for certain though. Whoever built this place didn't spare any expense."

"Do you think we can sneak in, Del?"

"Probably, but we're already trespassing. Best not to add breaking and entering to our list of crimes. Why don't we go to the courthouse and see if someone can tell us about the owners and if it might be for sale."

"You mean you might be willing for us to buy it, Del?"

"Maybe, Caroline, but we haven't even been inside to inspect it, and we have no idea if it's even available."

They continue to walk around the yard and sneak a few more peeks in windows. The more they look, the more excited they get. A loud crow caws overhead, and the young couple looks up and sees the house's magnificent tower reaching as high as the treetops.

"Oh my!" Caroline exhales. "I'd give anything for us to get up there and look around!"

"Uh huh," Delano agrees. "It's awesome and a little spooky looking. I bet it's got secrets!" he jests. "C'mon let's drive over to the courthouse and see what we can learn."

Chapter 3

THE PUTNUM COUNTY COURTHOUSE is an edifice whose architecture proudly exudes small-town stability. Its limestone construction looks like it could withstand a bomb blast while its glass dome gives visitors a sense that they can see into the heavens, and its large clock face is a metaphor that the county withstands the test of time. The courthouse is the heart of Greencastle's downtown, and the restaurants and merchants' shops surrounding it on cardinal points are its soul.

Caroline parks their Model T near the courthouse entrance on the north side of the square between another Ford automobile and a horse-drawn wagon whose main source of locomotion nibbles at grass at the side of the road.

The Engels exit their motorized vehicle, give the horse a pat on its rump, and walk inside the courthouse. Once inside they feel a cooler temperature due to the marble-lined interior and hear the faint echo of their footsteps as they approach the broad staircase leading to the county offices. They walk down a hallway and see a wooden and glass door with the words Recorder's Office painted in gold and black letters on translucent glass.

"Here we go, Caroline. I think this is where we should start." They open the door and see a room that looks like a library with shelves lined with leather-bound journals and books and aged maps of Greencastle and Putnam County adorning the walls. Four large wooden tables with green-shaded lamps are situated in the room for visitors to pore over books and documents. At the end of the room is a desk with a brass plate that reads Donnabelle McCabe, Recorder. The rest of the room is unoccupied with the exception of one notable character, an enterprising chap named Rice Foxx who is the owner and principal agent of Big Walnut Real Estate Company.

Delano and Rice recognize each other from a few local business luncheons and say hello. "Rice, I guess I shouldn't be surprised to see a real estate man in a recorder's office, and please excuse my manners, I'm not sure if you've ever met my wife, Caroline. She's not from Greencastle originally."

"I don't think I ever have. It's a pleasure to meet you, Mrs. Engel. I hope you've found our fair community to your liking."

"I do, Mr. Foxx. Greencastle seems like a cozy town, and Delano and I are still getting settled into the community since his return from the war."

"Well, if I can ever help you with any real estate needs, I hope you'll let me know."

They thank Rice and move on to speak with Miss McCabe who's staring intently at a stack of papers and books on her desk.

"Hello folks, I'm Donnabelle, how may I help you today?"

"Pleased to meet you. We're the Engels," Caroline says as she extends her hand to the recorder. My husband and I have found a property that we're a little intrigued with, but it's rather secluded, and it appears that it hasn't been occupied for some time. We thought we'd stop here to see if you or someone could share some information about it, you know, who the owner is and if it might be for sale."

From his perch at his table, Rice Foxx's ears perk up as he overhears Caroline's request.

"Well, Greencastle isn't that big so I suppose I might be able to help you. Can you tell me where the property's located?"

Delano answers, "It's just west of town on the way to the limestone quarry. We found it at the end of an overgrown grassy lane that led to a thick grove of walnut and locust trees. It's an old brick home with a carriage house."

"Hmm, let's take a look at the map of that area and see if we can find a plat number and the owner's name. Any idea how old the house might be? That'll help narrow down the record search."

"Well, we're not rightly sure, but it looks pretty old. It appears to be Victorian in design, so I guess from probably about the 1880s to just before the war, wouldn't you say, Delano?"

"Yeah, that seems right to me. It has a large carriage house and a roof tower."

"How'd you find it? You know, tucked away like you said."

Caroline beams and says, "We saw it from the air, well, the tower anyway and decided to go hunting for it."

"From the air?" Donnabelle asks quizzically. "Like from a hot air balloon or something?"

"From our aeroplane. Del and I own an aeroplane. Her name is Jenny!"

"Oh come down to earth!" Donnabelle jokes. "I've seen pictures of them aeroplanes, but I don't know that I'm ready for that sort of newfangled thing yet."

"Well, if you can help us with information about this property, maybe Del can take you up sometime."

"That's sweet, but I believe if God had meant for us to fly, He would've given us wings. No disrespect intended. Now then, let's see what I can find for you folks."

The three of them walk over to a county map on the wall dated 1900, and Delano points to the approximate location on the map, but nothing much appears but a large stand of trees. "I see the county road heading west from town toward the quarry, but nothing else except a few houses, woods, and farmland."

"A lot of times those older maps were more decorative than factually accurate. Let's check the real estate ledger for that specific area. If a house were built, it'll be there," Donnabelle says. She grabs a large ledger from the shelf and hefts it over to a table and begins leafing through pages. "Here it is, I think. It's called the Wright house, and like you said, Mr. Engel, it looks like it was built sometime in the 1880s."

"Any other information, like who the present owner is?" Caroline asks.

"Not that I see here," Donnabelle replies.

From his table on the other side of the room, Rice Foxx suggests, "You'll possibly quicken your search by looking at the county assessor's property tax records. When it comes to taxes, the government never forgets."

"You're right, Rice. Come with me, folks, we'll go next door and see our county assessor, Marvella Gooch. She likes a good challenge."

"Mind if I tag along, folks?" Rice inquires. "If you end up needing an agent, I'd be happy to help."

"Why don't you just cool your heels for a minute, Rice. You don't need to be trying to drum up business right now. I'm sure this couple will let you know if they need a real estate agent, okay?"

"Okey Dokey, just trying to help."

"Thanks, Rice, Caroline and I will let you know when we're ready. Right now we just want to find out some pretty basic information, but thanks," Delano adds politely.

The Engels and Donnabelle walk down the hall to the assessor's office where they meet Mrs. Gooch. Donnabelle explains that they're trying to locate the owner of what her records describe as the Wright property, just west of town.

Marvella Gooch is a serious-looking, middle-aged woman with wire-rim glasses and a double chin. "Gotcha, Donnabelle, let me see what we've got here." She begins going through some of her recent property tax records, and sees nothing. "Let me go back a little further in time and see what we come up with. Mr. and Mrs. Engel, you might want to take a seat. This could take a few minutes."

They do as she suggests, and Donnabelle says, "I'm gonna go back to my office and take care of a few things. I'll be there if you need me, okay?"

"Yes, ma'am," Caroline replies. "We sure appreciate your help."

About fifteen minutes later, Caroline and Delano hear Marvella declare, "Got it!"

The Engels sit up in their chairs waiting expectantly for the results of her search. "It appears that Christopher and Elizabeth Wright built the home in 1882 and paid taxes on the property until March of 1908. They are listed as owners of the Wright Lumber and Millwork Company which was located in the western part of the county. There's a notation from the probate court that they both passed away around the same time in 1908, and they died intestate, meaning there was no will. Apparently, the cause of the Wrights' death was never fully disclosed. Just says, 'cause unknown, mysterious circumstances.' So, unless I'm wrong, it would appear that the home was never sold and the estate was never fully closed."

"So, does that mean the property is available for purchase?" Delano inquires.

"Probably, but we'd need to get the county attorney to verify that. Looks like there's a history of unpaid property taxes, but otherwise my guess is, yes, that you could probably buy it if you were willing to pay the delinquent taxes also. Usually, the county would hold an auction for an unclaimed property, but since most people wouldn't want to pay the back taxes, and since we wouldn't even know about the house without you bringing it to our attention, I think our attorney would be willing to work with you on this. Plus, he's my brother-in-law, and I'll be happy to lean on him some. How's that sound?"

"Sounds good to us, Marvella! Any idea how much the taxes would be?" Caroline asks nervously.

Marvella takes a few moments to do her ciphering and says, "My best estimate is about $800."

"That's a lot of money, Del. What do you think?"

Delano nods his agreement. "Yeah, especially with the baby on the way and the new aeroplane. I've got some exciting thoughts about expanding our business, too, and that'll require some cash as well, but I think we can manage depending on the sale price, of course. I want us to talk with Rice Foxx a little bit about this since it's his area of expertise. Mrs. Gooch, you've been most helpful. We certainly appreciate you taking the time to look into this for us and your willingness to, uh, work with the attorney."

"My pleasure, folks, I hope it all works out for you and good luck with the baby."

Caroline takes Delano's arm as they walk back into Donnabelle's office. Rice Foxx is still sitting at the same place at his table poring over a plat book.

"Rice, if you've got a few minutes, Caroline and I would like to discuss some things with you."

"Absolutely! Was Marvella able to shed some light on the house you're curious about?"

"She was, and now we want to get inside the house to inspect it, and then if things continue to look good, we'd like to hire you to work out details with the county and help close the sale. And, since we're the ones who found the house, and since there appears to be no living owner to dicker with, we'd like for you to be generous with the real estate fee you'd charge us. Are you game?"

"Of course I am, and I'm willing to go easy on the fee too!"

No one else is in the recorder's office except Donnabelle, so the three of them sit in a corner, and Caroline and Delano fill him in on the information that Marvella shared with them.

"You know, now that you mention the name Wright, I seem to remember that lumber company from my youth. Seems like it just up and closed one day, and that was it. Kinda unusual."

"So, if you've got some time now, why don't we head over there, and see if we can get inside?" Delano says.

Rice looks at his watch and says, "Let's do it. I'll follow you in my car."

Chapter 4

"JEEZ LOUISE! No wonder this place has never been found. It's definitely off the beaten path. I thought I knew every property in Putnam County, but this place escaped me. Congratulations for finding it."

"Well, Rice, you can thank our aeroplane for that. Without Jenny we never would've spotted it," Caroline replies. She points to the house's roofline and says, "It seems like that tower was just poking out of the trees like it wanted us to find it."

"C'mon," Delano says, "Caroline, why don't you try to see what's inside the carriage house. Rice and I'll walk around the property to see if anyone's around and look at the foundation, walls, and gutters. We'll wait for you before trying to get inside the house's interior, okay?"

Caroline jogs off in the direction of the carriage house and slows her pace as she approaches it. "What a grand little building you are!" She notices that the structure has a bit of Gothic-Victorian style, rather unusual, and its barn-red paint looks surprisingly fresh. She tries the door handle, but it is either locked or frozen in place from lack of recent use. She looks inside one of the windows and uses her sleeve to brush away a layer of dust. She sees that the interior appears empty, but she's determined to get inside to get a better look. She pushes at the window's crossbar and with effort manages to push the lower half of the window up. She moves a log over to give her more height, then leaps into the open space, with her tummy coming to rest midway through. A few more grunts and shimmies later, and she unceremoniously lands on the floor inside.

Lying on her back she sees sunlight poring through the windows and says, "Yes, you are, indeed, a lovely little building!" She gets up and looks around. The space is empty and relatively clean. She follows a stairway up into a partial loft area and sees an old steamer trunk. Its surface is covered with colorful patches and travel stickers from countries all over Europe. England, Holland, France, Germany, Italy, Switzerland. "You folks certainly took some grand adventures, didn't you?" she says softly. She opens the wooden trunk expecting to find some fascinating treasures, but it's empty.

She shifts her gaze outside through another window and sees Delano and Rice waiting for her, so she takes a final look around the interior and heads off to join them. This time she unlocks the carriage house door and exits more gracefully. As she's standing in the doorway, she feels a rush of wind that musses her hair, and she swears she hears what sounds like a faint voice breathing out, "Seek me..."

Caroline dismisses the strange sound as wisps of wind and jogs off again to join her husband.

"What'd you find? Any interesting carriages or wagons?" Delano asks. "Maybe some tools or spare lumber?"

"No, nothing really interesting other than an old trunk up in the loft. It had a lot of travel stickers on it, so the Wrights apparently enjoyed traveling to Europe, but that's about it. I adore the building though!"

"Well, Rice and I looked around the exterior of the house, and it appears to be pretty darn sound. My guess is those old wooden box gutters will probably need some work, but otherwise, we didn't spot any major flaws that would be deal breakers on buying it. I think I know a way into it without forcing the door or breaking a window."

He grabs a lantern he brought from the trunk of the Model T and leads them to the rear of the house and points to the coal chute. "We're likely to get a little soiled entering here, but nothing ventured, nothing gained."

Caroline opens the door to the chute and says, "C'mon fellas, I'll lead the way." She hikes her skirt up a bit and slides inside. "It's kinda dark, but it's dry. C'mon down," her voice echoes up to the men.

Once inside Delano lights his lantern and the trio takes a few moments to let their eyes adjust to the dim light, and to see whatever there is to see. The first thing that Delano notices is that the basement has a stone floor unlike so many older houses that just have dirt floors. The next thing he notices is that the basement is bone dry and totally empty, not a scrap of old stuff that people usually relegate to the basement. There's no old furniture, no trunks with old clothes, no shelves filled with canning jars, nothing. The place is bare.

Delano leads them to a stout ash staircase leading up to an equally stout-looking wooden door. He tries the brass doorknob and it turns, but the door doesn't open until he leans his shoulder against it and pushes. The door relents to his effort, and Delano enters into the kitchen area. Caroline and Rice follow his lead, and the three of them stare in awe at the wonderfully crafted woodwork and overall condition of the Wright house.

"Wow! This place is something, certainly by Putnam County standards anyway," Rice remarks.

They begin exploring each room on the first floor. The kitchen cabinetry and counters are crafted of oak and ash, species hard enough to withstand daily use. The floor boards are six-inch wide oak planks, and the molding at the base of the floors is eight-inches high and made of ash. Decorative dental molding adorns the top of the walls where they meet the ceiling. The walls are whitewashed plaster and show a bit of soot discoloration where the stove ostensibly was, but otherwise, the kitchen looks in very good shape.

Caroline points to the arched pocket doors between rooms that are made of walnut. They're the first thing people would notice approaching the various sitting rooms. They enter what appears to be a study that has floor-to-ceiling walnut-and-cherry shelves. Here and there, they see carved cornices and light-colored maple inlay. On the floor by an exterior wall there is a stone pad where a wood stove rested, and the wall above it has a covered circular area where a stovepipe would've entered the chimney flue. Above each window frame is either a large pane of etched glass or brightly colored stained glass. The piece of stained glass above the front door proudly displays the name "Wright" with two doves on either side of the name.

As the trio goes room to room, they speak in low voices, as if in reverence to the rooms themselves, and to the people who made them. Caroline gives Delano a brief hug, and they both nod affirmatively to each other.

As they enter what appears to be the dining room, they see a magnificent crystal chandelier and a fireplace hearth and mantel made of sculpted marble. Delano holds his lantern up toward the chandelier and prisms of radiant colors dance upon the walls and ceiling. Caroline gasps in delight.

She leads the way upstairs, and they see four bedrooms and what appears to be another sitting room with its own marble fireplace and a cozy nook surrounded on three sides by curved glass windows. "Look, Delano, it's just off the master bedroom and could be a perfect room for the baby." He smiles at the thought.

They enter the large master bedroom and notice that it overlooks what appears to have been gardens and an orchard. The construction materials and designs in the bedroom are even more decorative than the other upstairs rooms.

"As I think about it," Delano begins, "it makes perfect sense that a couple who owns a wood-working company would install millwork in their home made from various species of fine hard-woods so they could show prospective customers the quality of work that the Wright Lumber and Millwork Company was capable of producing. It was Christopher and Elizabeth's home, but it was also a showcase of their capabilities and sensibili-ties." Caroline whispers to Delano, "It's so special, Del, let's make it our home."

Rice looks at his new clients, smiles, arches his eyebrows in admiration, and says, "We've got some very fine homes in our county, but I don't need to tell you that this property is unique, and you can own it."

Delano nods affirmatively, and Caroline says enthusiastically, "Let's go see the attic and the tower. I want to visit every inch of this place." And off they go, trekking up an enclosed wooden stair-way arriving in a large spacious room lined with cabinets and walk-in closets for storage of clothes, draperies, linens, and sundries. At the end of the room is another smaller room, above which the house's proud tower looms.

"Wow! What an incredible space!" Delano exclaims. "So much room. So much storage space, and look, Caroline, there's even a ladder leading to a landing and window near the top of the tower."

Delano and Caroline climb the ladder while Rice elects to stay below. The excited couple lean lovingly against each other as they look out of the tower's solitary window. "This is the home we want, isn't it, darling?"

Caroline smiles approvingly and a small tear of happiness comes to her eye. They peer out the window at the trees surrounding the house. They see a blue heron soar overhead much like they did in their Curtiss Jenny and hear the wind outside in the trees. They both close their eyes to listen and each hears a wavering rush of wind that almost sounds like a beckoning voice… "Find me…" and then it's gone, replaced by the normal sounds of wind in the trees. They look at each other with surprise.

"Did you hear something or someone just now?" Caroline asks.

"I thought so, too," Delano replies, "but it must be the wind. Don't you think?" They listen a little longer but only hear the wind.

"Funny thing is," Caroline says, "I heard a similar sound when I was in the carriage house. Weird, huh?"

"Yeah, weird. I think we must be a little overly excited at the prospect of buying this home."

Caroline and Delano descend the ladder and rejoin Rice in the attic whose been opening drawers and closet doors. "Everything is empty."

The trio walk downstairs to the front door and unlock it. "No sense getting all sooty climbing out of the coal chute," Caroline says. They take a final admiring look around the entry hall and step out onto the front porch. A stone sculpture of an angel greets them as they walk into the yard.

"So, what do you folks think?" Rice asks expectantly.

Caroline looks at Delano, and he replies, "We're definitely interested. We'd like for you to represent us and make an offer on our behalf. Caroline and I will let you know how high a price we're willing to pay. We're, of course, willing to pay the back taxes, too, and we'll pay in cash if that helps facilitate the process."

"Cash!" Rice replies. "Well, that should quicken the process instead of trying to get a bank loan. Why don't you stop by my office tomorrow, and I'll have our agency contract ready for you to sign, and you can tell me the price you're willing to offer. I'll be more than happy to work with the county officials to make this happen. Heck, you've already made friends with Donnabelle and Marvella. Their support will go a long way. How's that sound?!"

"Sounds excellent, Rice. Shall we say around three o'clock in your office then?"

"I'll be ready...and thank you." Rice walks back to his automobile and slowly pulls away. He looks in his rearview mirror and sees the Engels with their arms around each other looking at the wonderful Victorian mansion they're about to purchase.

"Cash, huh?!" Rice whispers out loud. "Well, I reckon if they've got enough to buy a house...and an aeroplane...there's probably a lot more where that came from."

Chapter 5

A T FIVE MINUTES BEFORE three o'clock the next day a bell tinkles on its doorframe as Caroline and Delano enter the offices of the Big Walnut Real Estate Company across from the courthouse in downtown Greencastle.

"Ah, you must be the Engels!" the receptionist, Heather Bee, says warmly as she rises out of her chair to greet the young couple. "I'm so happy to meet you!"

"Yes, Miss Bee, I'm Caroline and this fine gent is my husband, Delano. It's a pleasure to meet you as well. We believe Mr. Foxx is expecting us."

"Yes, indeed, he is!" comes an enthusiastic male voice as Rice sashays into the room. "Please step into my office. Perhaps you'd like a cup of coffee or tea as we go over the paperwork."

The Engels politely decline, and Rice closes his office door after the couple is seated at a round walnut table.

"So, Rice, have you had an opportunity to speak with the county's attorney about our interest in the property?"

"I have, Delano, and like me, Abe Zelensky was very much surprised that the property even existed, and upon his review of the tax and probate records, he was equally surprised that the estate was never fully settled. He said that in this day and age oversights like that were quite rare. Abe and I met last evening and again this morning in his office, and he agreed with Marvella's calculation that the delinquent taxes come very close to that $800 figure."

"Well, that's very good news, Rice, do you foresee any obstacles to our purchasing the property once we agree on the price?" Caroline inquires.

"No, not really, and neither does Abe. It appears that Christopher and Elizabeth Wright had a distant cousin residing in Sisseton, South Dakota. Abe called their county offices up there early this morning, and apparently the cousin had died in an accident in 1898 while trapping muskrats, of all things. There appear to be no other living relatives. The county clerk remembers it well because it was big news back in the day."

"That's terrific, Rice. I mean, not the cousin's death or the muskrats, but please tell us what comes next in this process, and when can we expect to close on the property?"

"Let's get to that in a moment please, Delano, I'd like to make certain that we have a complete understanding of what you're purchasing."

The trio takes the next few minutes poring over the description of the land and the structures on the property. "While the $800 in back taxes sounds high, I can assure you that if the property was reassessed for tax value today, it would be even higher.

Prices have jumped since the end of the war, with men returning with some bucks in their pockets. You can probably expect those taxes to increase within a year or two. Just so you know."

"Yeah, I can see that happening," Delano agrees, "but Caroline and I are prepared to move forward. You're the real estate expert, Rice, what do you think would be a reasonable offer for us to make? We have a limit on how much we're willing to pay, but we'd like to get your opinion."

"I asked that very same question of Abe to see if the county had set a minimum price that they'd accept. Abe told me that he wasn't going to lead with a price. He asked me to ask the Engels what they're willing to pay. My professional opinion is that you could probably get it for under $6,000. I recommend that we offer $4,800 and listen to what Abe says, okay?"

Caroline and Delano look at each other for affirmation. "What other expenses could there be beside your commission?" Caroline asks.

"There'll probably be a fee to do a title search, but it won't be much. Probably under $50, especially since Donnabelle and Marvella have already done much of that work. Now, let me make certain I heard you correctly yesterday when you said you didn't need or want a bank loan. Is that correct?"

"You did hear me correctly, Rice. We prefer to pay for the home with cash. I don't wish to have any debt. I've alerted our family's banker in Chicago, Mr. Zyer, that we're close to closing on a home, and he's assured me that we have ample resources to do it. He just needs a formal request from us and instructions for transferring the money to the proper authorities in Putnam County."

"Ah, very simple, very easy! The very best kind!" Rice gushes.

"I hope you don't mind my asking," Rice continues, "but I don't recall you saying what you do for a living. It's not everyone who can pay cash for a house after all, and you mentioned you're thinking about expanding a business here too."

"You're right, Rice, I didn't mention what I do for a living, and I prefer not to discuss my future business plans until I have things fleshed out a bit more. I'm sure you understand. As far as where our assets come from, let's just say that I inherited a bit of money and our families own manufacturing companies, principally in the munitions industry and clothing business. When the war broke out, well, we benefited."

"Impressive and enviable!" Rice voices. "Must be nice."

Caroline brought the subject back to the house. "So, when will we hear from you next, Rice, about the closing? With the baby due in a few months, we'd love to move in and begin getting things ready."

"Should happen pretty quickly I think, once we finish the price negotiations with Abe Zelensky, and your bank transfers the money to the county's account. I'll let you know as soon as I hear, okay?"

"Thank you, Rice, I'll speak with Mr. Zyer again once we finalize the negotiations. He assured us the transfer would occur smoothly. You know how to reach us."

With the meeting over he and Caroline stand to leave the office. They say goodbye to Heather who they see is reading a book entitled *Modern Nursing*. The bell tinkles again as they step through the door and onto the sunny courthouse square.

"Nice people," Heather remarks to her employer. "Yeah, and apparently very well off too."

The next couple of days are very exciting for Delano and Caroline. They stop by the Wright property again but choose not to enter the grand Victorian home or the carriage house until the purchase goes through. They walk around the property and find another piece of stone sculpture at the edge of the garden. It's a sweet headstone for a dog named Shadow.

"Everything and everyone comes and goes," Delano says softly. The war had taught him that. Caroline gently touches his cheek and says, "Our baby will bring us all a fresh beginning. I prefer to think the Wrights would be pleased to have the chatter of a little one in their home."

"Me, too, darling, but you know there are a couple of things I just can't quite figure out. For one, where did all of their furniture and personal household belongings go? They didn't have any close relatives to leave things to. Who cleaned out the place, and how did they die? It's all a bit of a mystery, and I guess we'll never know the answers."

"Good questions, Del. We may never know, but at least there's not a lot of old stuff we have to get rid of. What else are you wondering about?"

"The sounds we heard in the wind. What you heard at the carriage house, and what we thought we heard in the tower. It sounded so real, so human."

"Yeah, it was definitely unusual, and like you said, Del, we may never know, but here's what I do know. It's a lovely warm spring day. I was thinking that we might want to take Jenny up into the air again and see whatever other surprises we might find. Doc Kissel says we should enjoy the freedom while we can. Plus, I doubt how well I'll fit into the cockpit as you-know-who continues to grow."

"It is a beautiful day, and that sounds like a great idea. Perhaps you'd like to try your hand with the controls! I've got a feeling that we'll have two aviators in our family before too long."

"Really?!" she chirps, "But what if I get confused or I get smacked by a bird?" she laughs.

"Not a problem, darling, I'll have your back. Jenny has dual controls because she was designed for training. I bet Brian has her fueled up and ready for takeoff. I'm delighted that you like the wild blue yonder, too, because that's where I see our new business soaring. Civil aviation and more advanced instrumentation. It's the wave of the future, and we're fortunate to have the manufacturing capabilities from our other companies already in place."

Chapter 6

TWO DAYS LATER DELANO receives a phone call from Rice Foxx. "I'm very pleased to tell you that your first offer has been accepted. You're fortunate that you came in with a lowball price. I think that Abe is just happy to have some closure on this property, and I imagine that Donnabelle and Marvella urged him to help you out with the baby on the way. It appears that everything is in order with the exception of you and Caroline signing a few final documents which we can do in my office at your convenience. It would probably be a good idea to have a locksmith come out to change the locks and make sure your home and carriage house are secure. I'll be happy to arrange that if you wish."

"That's wonderful, Rice, and it would be great if you could handle the locksmith for us. Just let us know what we owe, and yeah, Caroline and I will stop by your office, say, around eleven o'clock tomorrow morning to finish things up if that time works for you. Let me also know what we owe for your commission."

"Will do, and yes, eleven would be fine. Thank you." After they hang up, Rice stares briefly at the phone. "Jeez, who's got that much money that they can buy a home without a bank mortgage? Sure wish I felt that flush."

The days that follow feel like a whirlwind to Delano and Caroline between closing on the house, going to her doctor's appointments, Delano moving his business plans forward, ordering carpets, drapes, and furniture, and, of course, buying an assortment of colorful items for the nursery. Then, too, there's yard work and the endless dusting and cleaning they're doing throughout their old house that lay vacant for so many years. Despite all of that, they still make time to visit the hangar regularly and have Jenny carry them aloft on new adventures. Before long, Caroline becomes quite adept as an aviatrix, and Delano feels confidence in her handling the takeoffs and landings.

And, the days stretch into weeks, and then a few more months pass. "Whew! Climbing these stairs is getting a bit harder these days, Del. I'm beginning to feel like a fat goose waddling along. Thank goodness we only have another few weeks to go before the stork arrives. I'm really glad that we only have the attic left to clean, but I think my climbing on ladders is about to end for a while."

"You have done so well with your pregnancy, sweetheart, but please let me do the climbing up on things from this point on. Agreed?"

"Yes, agreed. I hate feeling like I shouldn't do certain things, though. Perhaps after the baby comes we can hire a nurse for a little while and a housekeeper to help with chores."

"We'll do whatever you want, my love."

Caroline carries a broom and dust cloths up to the attic while Delano totes a ladder and buckets of water and cleaning supplies. "We're getting close to finally being done," she says. "We should be finished in another day or so, don't ya think, Del? My back is beginning to hurt, and I'm starting to feel a certain someone kicking me. I'm thrilled we're having a baby, but I'd view it as a personal favor if you had the next one, love!" Delano gives his beautiful, blushing wife a warm embrace. "You realize, of course, we still haven't settled on the baby's name."

"I know. I think I'm waiting for inspiration. Let's work on that tomorrow, shall we? But, for now we've got cleaning to do, and it'll be dark before too long."

Delano climbs the ladder and begins dusting the eight-inch wooden crown molding near the ceiling. After dusting he washes the boards and applies a layer of wax to help revitalize the old woodwork. He works his way over toward the entrance to the tower room and notices that there's an eighteen-inch wide area that sticks out a few inches further than the rest of the molding.

"Hmm, that's curious," he says, and Caroline looks up to his perch on the ladder.

"What is?" she asks. Delano climbs off the ladder to reposition it closer to the protruding area and reclimbs the ladder. "There's a cavity of some sort behind the molding here." He slips his fingers inside, expecting to find an old squirrel or bat's nest when he feels something smooth and flat and pulls out a very old looking collection of letters tied with a faded silk ribbon. "I'll be damned. Look at this, Caroline!"

"Wow, what did you discover, Del? Some secret treasure, I hope. Come on down here, and let's take a look. We could use a break anyway."

Delano steps off the ladder and joins Caroline who is now sitting on the floor with her back resting against an attic wall. He lays a small collection of envelopes between them, and Caroline gently unties the frayed silk ribbon binding them together.

"They're letters," she says, "and from the looks of them, they're quite old." Some of them have floral designs. Maybe they're old love letters that the Wrights sent to each other, and look here, a couple are from Holland. That would make sense since that old steamer trunk in the carriage house is covered with travel stickers from European countries."

They lean against each other, and as the sun gets lower in the sky, Delano lights a candle to help them to read. "This one's from Christopher to Elizabeth Arlene, and it's postmarked 1878." She takes a moment to begin reading it and smiles at the wonderful sentiments expressed.

My Dearest Elizabeth,

I hope this letter finds you doing very well, and that you know that I miss you dearly and cannot wait until we are together again. It seems impossible that we were together just a brief time ago and now you are so far away with your family.

I hope that you are enjoying your travels in Holland with your Dutch relatives and that you will return safely to me and in good spirits.

I have been quite busy getting my lumber company started, and with hard work and good fortune, I believe that I will soon be in a position to ask your father for your hand in marriage.

Upon your return I would very much enjoy selecting an engagement ring with you and looking for a lovely secluded sylvan site on which to build our home and our future together. I bid you safe travels and Godspeed.

With so much love, your devoted admirer!
Christopher

"Oh, Delano! That is so sweet, but I feel like we're voyeurs trespassing on their intimate moments." She winks at her husband coquettishly and says, "But, let's see what else they wrote to each other. I can't believe you found these, and I wonder why they were hidden away."

"This one's from Elizabeth to Christopher, and it's postmarked a couple of weeks after his."

My Darling Christopher,

It was so wonderful receiving your lovely letter. It does seem like eons since we were together, and yet I feel my love for you growing more and more with each passing day. I am so pleased to hear that your lumber business is doing well. I'm certain that Father will be equally impressed. He and Mother have asked me if I think we will wed, and I must confess that I blush when I tell them that I believe we shall.

My visit with our family in The Hague has been very enjoyable and Holland is fascinating. I believe this is the fourth time we have been on holiday with them, so they all feel very much like family. Fortunately, I have cousins that are within a couple of years of my age so I have fun times with them.

My older cousin, Vee, is a very talented artist which is only natural coming from such a cosmopolitan family of art dealers.

Please continue to write. I so look forward to hearing from you, and I promise to write you quickly in return.

In a few more weeks we shall catch a steamship for New York and then the train trip home to you in Greencastle. Know that I adore you and can't wait to be in your arms again…and then evermore. Yours in love eternally, Elizabeth

"Oh, Delano, they were so much in love and got married, then they built this house and had a thriving business. I wonder what else we can discover about them. I hope they enjoyed a wonderful life!"

"Look here, Caroline, it's another letter from Elizabeth to Christopher postmarked about two weeks later."

Dearest Christopher,

Hello, darling, our visit with our Dutch relatives is almost over. We depart by steamer tomorrow for New York and then the long train ride home to you. I can't wait!

Yesterday, we had a very interesting visit from an uncle whom I recall only meeting once years ago when I was a little girl. From all of the family lore that I remember over the years, Uncle Andreas was viewed as a recluse and had a reputation for being a mystic. I never quite knew what that meant, but yesterday he just showed up at the house and shared some unusual stories. He is quite old now and apparently not well, and I think he wanted to

*reconnect with the family and share his senti-
ments and mystical beliefs before it was too
late. It was sad in some ways, although his
spirits seemed positive and bright.*

*Near the end of his visit he pulled me aside
and said he had something he wanted to share
with me as a wedding gift. I don't recall any
of us saying that I would be getting married
soon, but he seemed to think that it was a
foregone conclusion. He gave me a leather-
bound book. It's very, very old looking, and he
said that it was given to him by a descendant
of the Tamberg Magical Dynasty and that it
held the power to tell of things to come. The
curious thing is that when I opened the book,
all of the pages appeared blank. Even more
curious...when I turned to ask him why the
pages were empty, he was gone! I looked in the
other rooms for him, but no one knew where he
was. It was the strangest thing, but my Uncle
Henk said that was typical of Uncle Andreas,
just being his typical eccentric self. I'll show
you the book when I return.*

So, my love, I shall see you soon, but not soon enough to suit me. I send you my undying love...Elizabeth

"Wow!" Delano exclaims. "That is a very strange story. I wonder whatever happened to the book!"

They continue looking through the little stack of letters, and Caroline finds another one from Holland. "It's from Elizabeth's cousin, Vee. It's postmarked about a year after the correspondence between Christopher and Elizabeth."

My Dear Cousin, Lizbet,

It was so wonderful sharing our family time together last summer at The Hague. I recently learned of your engagement to Christopher, and I couldn't be happier for the two of you. You were very sweet to send me an invitation to your wedding, and as much as I would love to attend and meet Christopher, my studies in Amsterdam and my modest purse make that difficult at this time. I hope that you will please forgive me.

*In my stead, I am sending you a wedding
gift of one of my recent paintings. Perhaps
the scene will remind you of the happy times
we cousins shared together. I hope it arrives
in fine condition and that it pleases you and
Christopher.*

With much fondness, Cousin Vee

"Aww, that was very thoughtful of Elizabeth's cousin," Caroline remarks. "I wonder whatever happened to the painting."

"Another mystery, darling, just like our wondering whatever happened to the rest of the Wrights' belongings. Perhaps we should look for other hiding places and more surprises."

"Yes, Del, but not tonight, I'm very tired now, and tomorrow's another day. Let's go downstairs to bed, and we can finish up in the morning, okay?"

Delano assists Caroline to her feet and places his arm around her waist to help steady his blooming wife. "Yes, my love! 'To sleep, perchance to dream.'"

Chapter 7

THE NEXT MORNING DELANO AWAKES early and quietly slips out of bed so he doesn't disturb Caroline's sleep. He puts his robe on and makes his way downstairs to the kitchen and prepares a pot of coffee. While waiting for it to brew, he steps outside onto the porch and is greeted by a pale reddish sunrise. "Rosy-fingered dawn," he whispers to himself as he recalls the ancient line from Homer's "Iliad."

He returns to the kitchen and pours himself a steaming cup of coffee and returns outside. He pulls his robe tighter around his torso to fend off the morning chill and walks into the yard. The stone statue of the angel greets him like a silent sentinel, and Delano looks at its visage and wonders if it's meant to represent someone the Wrights knew or if it's simply a decorative feature in the garden. He notices that one of the angel's wings is pointing up in the air, and he directs his gaze in that direction. It appears to be pointing at the house's tower.

"Of course you're pointing up!" he laughs. "Where else would an angel be pointing?" he quips. Delano sips his coffee and looks at the outline of the tower and sees that an area is covered in English Ivy. A sturdy scaffold is still erected from his earlier work on the box gutters, and he takes a final sip of his now tepid coffee and decides to climb the scaffold to get a better look at yet another project that he'll likely have to do.

From below, he hears Caroline's voice, "What in tarnation are you doing up there in your robe, Mr. Engel?"

"Good morning, sweetheart, I didn't want to wake you so I decided to come outside and begin my day without disturbing you."

"Well, I can see clear up to your knickers, sir! Aren't you chilly?"

"Yeah, it's a little breezy, but I saw ivy covering this part of the roof tower, and I decided to see if it's affecting the roof tiles in a problematic way."

"And, what is your assessment, my love?"

"Well, it appears okay," as he uses his hands to spread the ivy for a closer look. "Hey, Caroline, there's a small window here that I don't recall seeing before. Do you remember it?" He points to the area.

"There's that window in the tower that we've looked through before."

"No, this one's different, I think. It's smaller." He uses his hands again to spread the leaves to peek inside, but the ivy is old and stubborn. "I'm gonna need to bring a clippers up here to snip away the vines."

"Well, I'm getting cold standing out here in my bed clothes. Why don't you come down now, and we'll fix breakfast? We still need to finish cleaning the attic and tower room today, and you'll have plenty of time for this project later, okay?"

"Okay, sweetheart, but it's a little curious, don't you think?"

After breakfast they dress and return to the attic to finish what has been a lot of cleanup work for a large home that has sat untouched for a very long time. It's taken weeks to do a thorough job, but they're almost done.

"I can't get over those letters we found, Del. They really helped put some personalities to people who'd previously only been names. I wonder what happened to them, why they closed their lumber business, and why they seemed to vanish into thin air along with their worldly possessions."

"We may never know, and I'm curious why they hid the letters where they did. The mysteries surrounding Christopher and Elizabeth Wright just keep growing."

They work late into the afternoon and finally Caroline declares, "I think we're finished, Del, at least I am."

"You've been a real trooper! I'm pretty darn tired of doing this too. Why don't you just sit on this comfy chair I brought up for you? I want to get some clippers and see if I can remove those ivy vines, then I'll come back up. I won't be gone long, I promise."

"You'll get no argument from me. See you in a bit."

Delano sets his cleaning supplies down and helps Caroline get settled into a comfortable position. Then he heads down the stairs.

He finds his garden shears on the porch and ascends to the top of the scaffold. The afternoon sun makes his work easier by casting a warm light on the area where he viewed the window through the vines.

"There you are," he says softly, and he begins snipping away. A dove takes flight from its hidden nest and nearly causes him to lose his balance, but he keeps clipping the ivy. In a minute he's accomplished what he'd set out to do. He shades his eyes from the bright sunlight and peers inside. Lo and behold he spies another room that neither he nor Caroline had been aware of, despite their fastidious cleaning of the attic. He steps back from the window and tries to determine exactly where the room is inside the attic. He surmises that there must be an entrance in the tower room that possibly hides a room tucked in behind one of the cedar closets. He peers into the room again to try to confirm his reasoning, then alights down the scaffold and comes running up to join Caroline.

"There's a hidden room somewhere!" he announces breathlessly when he reaches the attic.

"You're kidding, Del, we've been over every inch of this place, and neither of us spotted anything to suggest that."

"I know, I know, but I saw it after I cleared the vines away."

"Here, help me up, and let's look together. Where do you think the entrance might be?"

"If my thinking is correct, there must be a hidden doorway in one of the closets next to the entrance to the tower room." Together they enter one of the closets and examine it thoroughly looking for any break in the molding or a dip in the floor, anything that would suggest unusual construction.

"Nothing!" Delano surrenders. "Do you see anything, Caroline? It must be here somewhere."

"I'm as befuddled as you are, Del, let's try the cedar closet."

They approach the closed door of the cedar closet like a pair of nervous interlopers. Caroline turns the doorknob and pulls open the door. The hinges squeak from a lack of use, and the couple cautiously steps inside. The walk-in closet measures approximately eight by eight feet and is lined entirely with aromatic cedar; floor, walls, ceiling.

Delano lights the candle he'd brought upstairs to the attic yesterday, and angular shadows dance along the interior with each movement he makes.

"Looks empty to me, Del. Maybe there's an entrance from the tower room."

"Maybe, but I'd swear it seemed to be positioned behind one of these two closets." Undaunted, he begins examining every inch, every board, every crevice until he feels like he's exhausted his search. "Dammit!" he bellows. "It must be here somewhere, and that's when they both hear a sound, barely a whisper, *"Find me, you're near..."*

They both look at each other incredulously and begin pressing on wall boards and molding strips, until at long last Caroline presses a cedar knot in one of the wall boards at the rear of the closet, and they hear an audible click, and a wall panel moves forward ever so slightly.

"You did it, love!" Delano slowly slips his fingertips behind the wall panel and gently pulls it forward. The panel swings open on silent hinges and reveals a hidden room behind the cedar closet, just as Delano had suspected. Sunlight streams into the room from where he'd cleared away the vines, and they both peer inside and gasp in surprise. The room is totally empty with the exception of an old oak rolltop desk that sits in majestic silence in the center of the illuminated room.

"Oh my!" Caroline exhales in stupefaction. "First the letters, and now this!" She clasps Delano's hand, and together they slowly approach something they never expected to find in a million years.

The afternoon sunlight casts a warm glow on the golden oak desk giving it a majestic appearance. The rolltop is closed, and they circle the desk respectfully as if it might come alive at any moment.

Caroline opens a few of the drawers on the desk's double pedestals and then tries the central pencil drawer. Each drawer is empty, just like every closet and drawer was in the house when they bought it.

Delano reaches his hand out and slips his fingers inside the bottom of the rolltop and gently lifts the tambour revealing several cubbyholes and more drawers. But, what captures their attention the most is a very large, green leather-bound book resting alone on the desk's writing surface.

"Oh my!" Caroline expresses again. "The surprises just keep on coming!"

Delano gently opens the ancient-looking book and sees that all of the pages are blank. There's not a single word anywhere throughout the entire tome except inside the front cover and on its spine. Engraved in gold letters are the words:

Ex Libris Tamberg

"Of all things why would they hide a desk and a big blank book in their attic? It doesn't make any sense to me. Does it to you, Del?"

"Caroline, your guess is as good as mine, but it's becoming obvious that there's more to this property than meets the eye."

They open a few more drawers as if expecting different results from the empty ones they've already seen, but the old rolltop is void of anything except the green leather book.

"Sweetheart, we're about to have a baby, and I'm beginning to feel more than a little nervous about all of this. Do you think it's safe here? Maybe there's a reason why this house wasn't found for many years."

Caroline and Delano look at the open book again, then hear a stirring sound in the attic, and words begin to suddenly appear in a deep, rich script on the blank page before them.

*This is your home and you
and your baby are safe.*

Chapter 8

DELANO SITS ON THE FLOOR next to Caroline and cradles her head in his lap. Upon seeing the words magically appear in the old book, she passed out, slumped in his arms, and he gently lowered her to the floor.

"Caroline! Sweetheart, are you okay?" He lightly brushes her disheveled hair from her face and softly strokes her cheek. "Caroline, are you okay?" he tries again. A moment later her eyes flutter open, and she looks into Delano's eyes.

"Del, what am I doing down here?" she asks in confusion.

"You fainted, honey." And then she remembers, and her eyes squint shut. "Please tell me that didn't really happen, Del? Please tell me that book didn't actually communicate with us."

"C'mon, darling, why don't you try to stand up, okay?"

"But, Del, didn't we just see words appear where a second ago there were none?"

"Yes, I believe we did."

The couple stand up together and stare in bewilderment at the old green leather-bound tome. The words that suddenly appeared a few minutes ago are gone.

"How is this possible, Del? Things like that don't just happen, do they?"

"Not that I'm aware of, Caroline, but I wouldn't have expected us to find old letters that were hidden behind crown molding either, or a rolltop desk in a secret room in the attic…or, words that we both heard in the wind and can't explain." They stare at the book again, and Caroline begs the question, "How is any of this possible?"

And, again, as if by magic, words appear in the book:

You have been chosen to know and protect my secrets

"What are you?" Delano asks plaintively.

I am the sum knowledge of the Tamberg Magical Dynasty

"Why were we chosen, and how can a book with blank pages make words appear, and why are you here in our house?" Caroline asks.

Answers will come to your questions in good time. For now, know that I am here to help guide you.

Visit me here from time to time
and tell no one about me
Lest my silence seal your fates.

"What the hell does that mean? Seal our fates!" Delano challenges. "And who in God's name are the Tambergs? Caroline, this has to be some sort of silly parlor trick which I don't find particularly amusing. Words can't just suddenly appear. C'mon, I've read enough of this rubbish for one day."

They begin to leave the room and head downstairs when they hear a flutter of pages from the book.

There is no reason to fear my words.
I am here for you when you need me.

The shaken couple walk down the steps to their bedroom and close the door to the attic. Caroline and Delano clean up and climb into bed. They lie side by side in the dark in silence, each trying to process what has occurred.

"Are you awake, Caroline?"

"Wide awake, Del. I can't seem to turn off my brain."

"Yeah, me neither. I just don't understand how any of this is possible. I mean, we're both fairly rational people, but this doesn't come close to making any sense."

Caroline snuggles next to her husband. "I know, Del, but let's try to put it behind us for now, okay? I'm totally exhausted, and I'm trying to stay healthy for the baby."

He agrees. "We can talk in the morning." Secure in each other's arms, they eventually fall into a deep sleep...and Delano dreams...about people he doesn't know in a land across the sea. In the dream he sees an odd, older man approach a young lady around his age with an antiquated green book that he gives to her as a wedding gift. She brings the book back to America, to this very house, and it's remained here ever since as a spirited sentinel. The woman's name is Elizabeth, and she and her betrothed, Christopher, are about to begin their lives together as husband and wife.

The next morning Delano awakes with the sunrise and quietly slips downstairs to the kitchen to make coffee. While it's brewing he steps outside onto the porch to watch the sun break through the trees and warm the chilly air. A few minutes later he hears Caroline moving around the kitchen and comes back inside to join her.

"How'd you sleep, sweetheart?" he asks as he gently touches her round tummy. "And you, too, little one?" he coos at Caroline's belly. "Did you have a good sleep too? Are you ready to come out and meet your parents? Soon, little one, very soon!"

"I slept okay, Del, but I had the strangest dream."

"Oh?! Me too."

Caroline proceeds to tell him about her dream, and he nearly spurts out his coffee in surprise as she recounts a dream that is remarkably similar to his.

"No way!" he blurts out. "I had virtually the same dream."

"You're not serious, are you?"

"Afraid so, love! Right down to the names of the couple that built this house and got that big dumb book." They stare at each other and shake their heads incredulously.

"Caroline, I think it might be a good idea for us to get away from the house for the day. We've spent a lot of time working on the place, and I think maybe the fumes from the cleaning supplies are starting to addle our brains. Why don't we go into town for some groceries and head out to the airport and take Jenny for a final flight before you give birth. How's that sound?"

"Sounds grand to me, Del, my due date for the baby is in a few days, so this'll be my last chance for us to fly together for a while."

"Roger that, darlin'. I think I'll drive this time too."

A few minutes later they're riding into town and park near the entrance to Barney's grocery store located a few doors down from the Big Walnut Real Estate office. "While we're here, Caroline, let's stop in and see Rice Foxx. I haven't paid him yet for the locksmith he sent out to change our locks."

The familiar bell tinkles as they enter the office door, and they see Heather Bee sitting at her desk, the top of which is strewn with nursing medical books.

"Well, if it's not the Engels. Greetings, folks! What brings you in today? Rice is on the phone right now, but I expect he'll be off the line shortly."

"Thanks, Heather," Caroline says. "From your books it looks as if you're gonna be switching your career from real estate to nursing, huh?"

"Yes, I've been taking nursing classes at Putnam County Hospital. Always wanted to be a nurse. Love babies, so I thought I might specialize in newborns and pediatrics. From the looks of it, you're about ready to pop, aren't you?" she gushes.

"Yeah, any day now. I may need to call on you for some help after the baby arrives if you're available."

"Sure, I think I could help you out if you're serious. I think I recall your mentioning that Doc Kissel is your physician, but yeah, I don't think Rice would miss me too much. He's been training my replacement for a little while anyway. Besides, Rice and I have grown rather close personally, and it would probably be a good idea for us not to be together twenty-four seven."

"Hmm, that's interesting. Well, I'm glad we decided to stop in. Delano and I'll talk, and I'll probably be back in touch with you very soon."

"Sounds good. I just love them little babies!" Heather peeks into Rice's office and says, "Well, I think he may be on the phone a little longer than I thought. Do you want me to tell him anything in particular?"

"Yes, please," Delano replies. "I brought him this check to reimburse him for the locksmith. Please tell him thanks, okay?"

"Will do, and you folks have a great day!"

Caroline and Delano exit the real estate office and go off to the grocery store. A few moments later Rice joins Heather, and she hands him the check.

"Oh, sorry I missed them. I have an extra set of door keys that the locksmith made. The Engels are a rather interesting couple. I still am mightily impressed by their apparent means. Paid cash for that big house."

"Well, Ricey Poo, I think you might be more jealous than impressed, huh?"

"Yeah, I reckon you're right. Some folks are just born into the right womb or get lucky or something." He lightly caresses Heather's neck. "Why don't you put the closed sign in the window for a bit and come into my office for some, uh, dictation?"

"Oh, Ricey!" she giggles. "You're such a bad boy!"

After picking up the groceries at Barney's, Delano drives their Model T out to the airfield. Brian greets them as usual and offers to put their perishable groceries in his ice box until they return from their flight.

"Yup, you're all fueled-up and ready to go! It's a gorgeous day, and you should be able to see for miles. I'll help you climb aboard Mrs. Engel, if you need assistance."

"Thanks, Brian, I think I'll be okay. I'm pregnant, not crippled!" she chides. With a little effort she manages to find a comfortable sitting position. "I guess I'm not going to get any style points for that entry, am I, Captain?" she shouts to Delano.

"You're the prettiest and most graceful girl on the planet!" he lobs back at her. "Let me know when you're totally situated, okay?"

A moment later she gives him a thumbs-up, and he motions for Brian to remove the wooden blocks holding the wheels, and to give the propeller a yank. Brian follows his cues, and Delano engages the throttle, and they begin rolling down the grassy runway. "Woohoo!" Caroline hollers which has become her customary shout whenever they lift off. Within a few seconds they're airborne, and they pass a small flock of Canada Geese as they climb above the rolling Putnam County countryside.

It is, indeed, a glorious day as they cruise from one puffy cloud to another. They again head west toward town, and Delano drops their altitude as they soar past Asbury College's campus and Gobin Methodist Church. In seconds they're upon the Carnegie library and then swoop down even lower to get a great view of the dome of the courthouse. People from the ground look up and wave, and then they're on to the countryside and the Dunbar covered bridge over Big Walnut Creek.

Caroline is in heaven. She tilts her head back and lets the sun radiate its warmth on her and the baby. Her silk scarf buffets in the wind, and she points for Delano to fly in the direction of the craggy limestone quarry where they love to walk. The quarry is populated with hikers who look so tiny, and Caroline laughs as she sees a fellow on a high-wheel bicycle tumble as he attempts to see their Jenny flying overhead. Caroline then points in another direction, and Delano knows that she wants him to cruise past their house. This time there's no surprise when they see the roof tower breaking through the surrounding trees. Delano flies a few wide circles around the roof and is surprised this time, though, as he notices a particularly bright golden light emanating from the window where the rolltop desk is located.

Caroline notices the unusually bright radiance, too, and turns in her cockpit to look at Delano. She sees him gesture as if to say, "Go figure!" A couple more circles around the rooftop and Delano pulls the Jenny away for their return to the airfield. He checks the hangar's windsock as he approaches to confirm wind direction, then lines the aeroplane up with the runway and sets her down. Brian is waiting for them as they approach the hangar, and Delano cuts the engine.

Delano jumps out of his cockpit and then helps Caroline as she squirms her way out of hers and down a ladder.

"How was it?" Brian asks Caroline.

"Grand as always and no traffic up there, except for a few birds!"

"Well, enjoy the empty skies while you can. I have a feeling that before too long aeroplanes will be everywhere."

"That's what I'm counting on," Delano replies. "At least, that's what my business plan is anticipating. The county's gonna need more acreage to accommodate the wave of commercial aircraft that's coming. You mark my words, Brian! You're going to be busier than you ever dreamed possible."

The Engels collect their groceries from Brian's icebox and place them in their Tin Lizzie. "Well, next time we see you, Brian, there's likely gonna be three of us."

"Yeah, looking forward to meeting the baby. Have you come up with a name yet?"

"It's a work in progress," Delano replies. "We have a few ideas depending on gender, but nothing has stuck so far."

"How about Brian?" The manager jests. "That's a rock solid name, or Brianna if it's a girl."

"We'll take your suggestions under advisement, sir!" Caroline lobs back at him.

They climb into the Model T and drive in the direction of home.

"You saw that bright light as we flew over the house, didn't you, darling?"

Delano looks at Caroline. "Yeah, you know we both did. No telling what's gonna be waiting for us when we get home."

Chapter 9

THEY ARRIVE HOME, exit the automobile, and both look up to the house's tower wondering if the radiant light they'd seen from the air is still glowing, but nothing special emanates. Caroline and Delano give each other a brief glance to acknowledge that they're wondering the same unsettling thoughts.

"Let's get these groceries put away, Caroline, and then we'll see how you're feeling, and what else you're up for doing today, okay?" She nods her agreement, and they begin unloading the car.

"Whew, I sure don't have the energy I once had, Del. I think it might be a good idea to speak with Heather Bee again about helping out. Are you comfortable with that?"

"That's fine with me. Why don't you contact her and make arrangements."

"Good, because I feel like I'm going to burst any minute! I think I'd like to lie down for a bit after we put the groceries away. I could use a nap."

"Why don't you lie down now in the guest room on the first floor so you won't have to climb the stairs? I can handle the groceries. I've even set up a makeshift cot at the foot of the bed so I can be close but won't disturb you."

"You are a prince, Mr. Engel! Perhaps I can dream up a name for the baby and not dream about, uh, weird things."

Delano helps Caroline get settled in the guest room and then finishes putting the groceries away. He walks outside into the yard and stares up at the little window where he'd pulled away the ivy vines.

"From here you don't look a house that's got a bunch of mysteries," he says to himself. He shakes his head in confusion and decides to take this time while Caroline's napping to ascend into the attic and revisit the old book. He climbs the steps and enters the cedar closet. He hesitates briefly, then pushes the knot in the wall. Like before, a cedar panel opens revealing the hidden room with the rolltop desk bathed in sunlight. "Whew, I hope I'm ready for this."

He approaches the beautiful oak desk and admires the intricately carved drawer handles and the cubby holes that show discoloration from years of use. The green book lies open in the center of the writing surface. Its antiquated pages are blank. Delano gently flips the pages one at a time. The only words he sees are on a book plate inside the front cover. They're the same as the gold engraved words on the spine. Ex Libris Tamberg...from the library of Tamberg.

He finishes flipping through the tome and sets it down as he found it with its pages open. "So, who is Tamberg?" Delano asks softly.

A moment later he's startled as words in a bold script begin scrolling onto the empty page.

The Tamberg Magical Dynasty

"Okay, now I'm communicating with a book again," he mumbles to himself as if trying to gauge his sanity. "Can you tell me about this Tamberg Dynasty?"

The book flutters several of its pages and words begin to appear.

The Tamberg Magical Dynasty were an upper middle-class Dutch family of magicians spanning six generations. The oldest children were trained as magicians and carried on the tradition to the next generation. Three were court magicians entertaining the royal family. They became adept at chemistry and necromancy and

had an uncanny ability to make
things appear and disappear.
The three most prominent
magicians in the family were
Hudson, Sawyer, and Atticus.
Their sum knowledge created
the book before you.
I exist solely to guide and serve you.

"Well, that's a relief!" Delano exclaims sarcastically. "Sure wouldn't want an old green book to be angry with me."

A response to his annoyance appears quickly.

No, you wouldn't!

"So, oh great wise book," Delano continues with sarcasm. "How do I know that you're not some parlor trick, and why did you write that my wife and I were 'chosen'?"

It is reasonable to ask if my presence and my words are a parlor trick since Hudson, Sawyer, and Atticus were the greatest illusionists of their day, and they did, indeed, employ trickery for their audiences. However, over the generations the Tambergs were able to transcend simple magic tricks. Through their eventual mastery of chemistry and necromancy, they learned to bend the laws of nature. They did eventually learn to change base metals into gold, and even more stupefying, they were able to bring the dead back to life...though not without dire consequences...

As to why you and your wife have been "chosen" to be the beneficiaries of my abilities, that is something that may be revealed in time. For

now, know that you are safe and
that your child will be well...
But, understand, too, that
there will be turmoil that your
family must face bravely...

Those final words rattle Delano to his core. "What if we don't wish to be 'chosen'? What if I want our family to live simple, happy, productive lives without the benefit of your, uh, guidance. Why not just choose someone else and leave us the hell alone?"

There is no immediate reply from the book, and its silence rattles Delano even more so. Then, the book's pages begin to flutter anew.

There are certain mysteries that lie
beyond what I can divine, from a realm
unseen. The Wrights asked the same
question after Elizabeth brought me back
from Holland. Perhaps someday this will

all become known to you, perhaps not. I am only here to help serve and guide.

"Speaking of Christopher and Elizabeth Wright, whatever happened to them, and where did all of their possessions go?"

To a realm unseen
With the exception of one item
that still remains...
A gift, verily, a Dutch treasure.
Ask me no more. That is all I
can share with you...for now.

"But, wait!" Delano stammers. "Surely, you can divulge more!" But, the spirited book from the library of the Tambergs remains silent, and Delano is left alone with his questions and his concerns. He waits a few moments longer but sees nothing further from the sentient book. He shakes his head in frustration, leaves the room, closes the cedar door panel, and descends the attic stairs to rejoin Caroline.

Chapter 10

"OH, THERE YOU ARE, Del, I was wondering where you were. I came into the kitchen to make some tea and thought you might be outside working in the yard. While I was waiting for you, I called Heather Bee and got her lined up to help us when the baby arrives."

Caroline notices a perplexing look on Delano's face. "Are you okay, sweetie? You look like you've just seen a ghost."

"I think maybe I have," Delano says cryptically. "While you were napping, I went to the attic to see if that book is just a big green book, or if…" His words trail off from there…

"Or if what?" Caroline prompts.

The couple sit down at the kitchen table, and Delano proceeds to tell his wife, chapter and verse, about his communication with the book. She sits stunned. "Now, I know why you look like you've seen a specter! It appears as if you have!"

"Craziest thing I've ever experienced! On one hand it's all a little frightening, with this thing about the Tamberg Magical Dynasty and the Wrights' disappearance. On the other hand I must admit that I feel intrigued by what this book can share, and what it chooses not to share. I have no idea what's coming next."

Delano notices an odd expression on Caroline's face, and all of a sudden her water breaks. "Oh boy!" he shouts as he leaps to his feet not quite sure what to do next. Caroline had planned ahead and already has a bag packed to go to the hospital. She tries to remain calm but is clearly going into labor. He runs into the bedroom to get her bag and his wallet, then helps his wobbly wife to her feet and guides her into the Model T.

"Now, take it easy, Del, I don't want you running off the road!"

"Yes, dear! Can you believe it we're having a baby, and we haven't even settled on a name yet?!"

"Uh, yeah, and it hurts like hell!"

Several minutes later they arrive at the ER at Putnam County Hospital, and Dr. Nita Barr begins an examination and asks questions about the timing of labor pains, etc. "Now, just try to relax, Mrs. Engel, you're in good hands here, and we've got a phone call into Dr. Kissel's office to let him know your status. He should be here shortly. And you, Mr. Engel, can go sit in the OB waiting room with all of the other expectant fathers."

Several hours later a disheveled looking Delano Engel is led back to a private hospital room where Caroline lies in bed cradling their little bundle of joy. He lightly kisses his exhausted wife on the cheek and peers at the new arrival.

"Say hello to your daughter, Del, isn't she just the most precious thing you've ever seen?"

"You both are, darling, as he bends down to get better acquainted with his daughter. "Oh my, she's so tiny and so beautiful! What shall we name her?"

"I was lying here holding her and watching the sunrise outside the window. I was thinking Aurora might be a lovely name. What do you think, Del?"

He can't take his eyes off of her. "I think Aurora would be a perfect name, just perfect! Hello, Aurora!" he coos at the baby. "I'm your papa!"

An OB nurse named Mossie enters the room and tells them that Doc Kissel thinks the delivery went fine and that the baby appears to be very healthy.

"Mrs. Engel, we're going to keep you and the baby here for a day or two just to help you regain your strength, then Mr. Engel can take you home after Dr. Kissel releases you."

"Thank you, Mossie," Delano murmurs, but he can't take his eyes off of his beautiful wife and daughter. "Hello, little Aurora," he coos again.

Two days later the Engel family pulls into their driveway and are met by Heather Bee who Delano had called and asked to meet them at home. Caroline carefully hands Aurora to Delano as she slowly moves to exit the Model T. Heather follows them inside and is giddy with excitement to see the baby.

"Oh my goodness, aren't you just the prettiest little thing!" she says as they slowly walk up the steps to the master bedroom and the nursery adjacent to it."

"Thank you for agreeing to help us, Heather. We've prepared a guest room for you for a couple of nights, and then we can discuss a schedule that we're all comfortable with, if that's okay with you."

"That would be fine, Mrs. Engel. We'll figure it out as we go along. Rice knows that I won't be in the real estate office for a few days, but first let's get you and the baby settled, okay? I'm excited to put my nursing studies to practical use."

As expected, the first couple of days are quite an adjustment in the Engel home. As talented a man as Delano is, he's learning a whole new skill set as a first time father, including the diaper changing thing.

Heather proves to be very helpful and occasionally takes on some additional duties with housekeeping and meal preparation. Within a week, though,

Caroline is fully recovered and proving to be quite adept as a new mother, so Heather's assistance is no longer required.

"I don't know how we could've managed without your great help, Heather. I hope you'll consider helping us again should we need you."

"Of course, Mrs. Engel, I've grown rather fond of little Aurora, and you and Mr. Engel can call on me anytime."

The days stretch into weeks and eventually a few months go by. While Delano is gone during the day establishing his commercial aircraft business, Caroline spends wondrous hours with Aurora in the garden, listening to music, or looking at picture books together in the carriage house. Caroline couldn't be happier, and the only time they're not together is when she puts the baby in the nursery for a long nap.

For Delano these are extremely exciting times. His love of flying has developed into the fully fledged business enterprise that he'd hoped. In addition to owning his Flying Jenny, he's either bought or supervised the manufacture of more sophisticated aircraft with more powerful engines capable of carrying larger and heavier cargoes. His company, Engel Air, now delivers the U.S. mail and commercial packages to several cities within a few hundred miles, plus crop dusting for farmers, and even sightseeing flights for thrill seekers. But, Engel Air's most lucrative business comes from manufacturing precision parts for the government's burgeoning defense industry.

And, with Putnam County being the small community that it is, it doesn't take long for the news of his business success to become well known. Engel Air quickly builds its labor force to some twenty designers, engineers, and craftsmen, putting the little town of Greencastle, Indiana, at the forefront of some of America's best aviation technology.

Caroline and Delano are so busy with their daily lives that even the thoughts of the unusual book have taken a back seat. They occasionally venture up into the attic to store or retrieve household items but never venture into the room hidden behind the cedar closet. The Tamberg book is a disturbing distraction that they choose to mentally tuck away for a while. Out of sight and out of mind...mostly, but not entirely.

———————

"It's Sunday, Del, and you've been working so hard. Please just stay home with me and Aurora today. Your work will be there waiting for you tomorrow, okay? Besides, Heather has agreed to come over soon to help out for a while so we can enjoy the day together."

Delano hugs his wife and gives her a tender kiss. "You know, darling, I was thinking that maybe we should think about having another baby before we get too much older."

"You're a randy beast, Delano Engel!" she teases her husband. "And, when do propose that we, uh, do what is necessary to make that happen?"

"Well, if Heather's going to be here, we could put Aurora down for a long nap and maybe sneak off to the carriage house for a little conjugal whoopee. We have that spare brass bed in there, and Heather can keep an eye on Aurora for a couple of hours. How's that sound, love?!"

"Sounds like a splendid idea, and I have a feeling that Aurora is suddenly becoming very, very sleepy."

"Now, who's the randy beast, you little vixen?!"

Chapter 11

SEVERAL MINUTES LATER Heather arrives at the Engels' home carrying a large satchel, and she and Caroline go upstairs to the nursery. Aurora is lying on her back in her crib playing with her favorite toy, a plush hedgehog.

"Ah, there you are my little angel. Have you missed your Auntie Heather?" She tickles her belly and Aurora gets the giggles. "My goodness, what

I wouldn't do to have a sweetheart of a child like her. You're a lucky woman, Mrs. Engel!"

"Yes, Delano and I thank our lucky stars every day to have such a happy and healthy child. So, if you're okay with this, Delano and I will be in the carriage house for a couple of hours. I know you're very accustomed to Aurora and where everything is, but if you need us, just let us know, okay? I'll lock the door on my way out."

"Will do, and I hope you and the mister can enjoy some alone time together. So, just be off with you now, and don't worry about a thing."

Caroline bends down and gives her baby a little peck on the cheek and leaves the nursery to join Delano. After she departs Heather reaches down in the crib and adjusts the baby's blanket to help keep her warm. She then goes to one of the curved glass windows in the nursery and looks out into the back yard. The yard has a very dense grove of trees that extends a long way. It's what helped keep the property secluded and private for so long. Heather stands at the window ostensibly eyeing the sylvan view. She remains there for several moments nodding her head up and down ever so slightly, then returns her attention to Aurora. As Heather's walking back to the crib she hears a rustling noise like the wind picking up. She finds it odd to hear that sound from within the house, then stops cold as she hears an unmistakeable scolding voice in the wind, "Noooo"…and then it's gone.

Meanwhile, Delano and Caroline putter around inside the carriage house. Over the past few months they've decorated it as a guest quarters and a play area for Aurora as she gets older. It has a wonderful horned phonograph made by Thomas Edison and a grand brass bed. At the foot of the bed is the old steamer trunk covered in travel stickers that the Wrights had left behind. They store extra sheets and blankets inside it. Caroline closes the louvered blinds and turns off a silk-shaded floor lamp. She draws Delano close to her and raises a leg around the back of his. They kiss for a few moments and Delano begins unbuttoning the front of her blouse. They slowly move over to the brass bed, completely disrobe, and fall beneath the covers enjoying the rhythmic feel of each other's body.

"My, my! Mr. Engel, you certainly know how to make a girl feel wanted."

He kisses her lightly and says, "Well, darlin', what's not to want?!" They lie in each other's arms for a brief period, enjoying their intimacy, then both drift off to sleep.

An hour later Caroline awakes and sees the time on their pendulum wall clock. She begins to get out of bed, and Delano draws her back beneath the sheets.

"My goodness, Del, you do want to have another baby, don't you?!"

"Of course I do, especially if we can have another one as perfect as Aurora. Twenty minutes later they finally manage to break free from their embraces, clean up, and get dressed.

"Well, sir, I wish to thank you for a most entertaining afternoon," she flirts, "but I think I'd better go and check on our daughter."

The satiated couple leave the carriage house and walk across the yard to their home's front porch. Caroline takes her key and inserts it into the door but sees that it's unlocked. "That's odd, I could've sworn I'd locked that door when I left Heather."

They enter their entry hall and walk up the stairs toward the nursery. The house is quiet. No sounds of Aurora laughing or Heather playing with the child. Caroline calls out, "Heather, we're back."

They step into the nursery and chills go down both of the Engels' spines. They see Heather lying on the floor in a heap, and the crib is empty. Aurora is gone.

Caroline gasps in horror as she rushes to the crib and quickly moves the baby's blanket hoping beyond all hope that she's simply under the covers. "Del, she's gone. Our baby's gone!" She immediately goes into their bedroom to see if she'd crawled away, but intuitively she knows that Aurora won't be there.

Delano kneels by Heather and gently shakes her shoulder to awaken her. "Heather. Heather, can you hear me? Wake up!"

Heather's eyes flutter open and in confusion she asks, "Mr. Engel, what am I doing down here?"

Before he can answer, Caroline asks frantically, "Heather, where's Aurora? She's gone. I can't find her anywhere!"

"What?" she stammers. "What do you mean she's gone? Ooh, my heard hurts."

Delano goes into the master bedroom and dials the operator. "We need the sheriff's office and a doctor. Can you please contact them? I believe some-one may have kidnapped our baby, and our sitter has sustained a head injury." He gives the operator his name and address. "Please hurry!"

Delano helps Heather into a chair and then wraps his arms around his sobbing wife. "Heather, do you have any idea what happened? Did some-one enter the house and hit you and then take Aurora?"

"I don't know, Mr. Engel. One moment I'm playing with little Aurora in her crib, and the next thing I know you're kneeling by me waking me up."

"Oh, Del, what are we going to do? We never should've left her. I want my baby!"

Delano does his best to comfort her, but he also feels guilty and disconsolate. "We'll get her back, sweetheart, I promise you."

A few minutes later they hear the shrill sounds of sirens as emergency vehicles approach the house. Delano rushes down the stairs to let them in. He's met by two uniformed officers, a plain clothes detec-tive named Buster Bodine, and a Dr. Clodfelter. The detective directs the two officers to do a thorough search of the premises, and he instructs the Engels and Heather to go into the master bedroom so as not to disturb the crime scene any further.

Fifteen minutes later Heather has been examined by the doctor who determines that she hasn't suffered a concussion, only a nasty bump on her head. And, twenty minutes after that the Engels and Heather have given the detective a full accounting of what they know. And then, a few minutes later the telephone rings.

Delano answers the phone with Detective Bodine listening closely nearby.

A muffled voice says, "Engel, we have your kid. You need to do exactly as I say if…"

Delano interrupts, "If you harm our child, I swear to you that I'll…"

"Engel, shut up and listen if you ever want to see your kid again in one piece!"

Delano remains silent. "Your child is safe, for now. I'll call you again in a little while with instructions. Do not call the authorities and do exactly as I say. Understand, Engel? If you do, you'll get your kid back. Stay by your phone." The line goes dead.

Delano stares at the telephone with frustration and anger etched on his face.

"What did he say, Del?" his distraught wife pleads.

"He said Aurora is safe and that he'll call back with instructions." Delano looks at Bodine. "Any bright ideas, Detective?"

"We wait for them to call back and take it from there. I know this is extremely frightening but it's the only course of action we have. Let me ask you, Mr. Engel, can you think of anyone who would wish your family harm? Any business associates, any relatives or former friends?"

"None that I can think of. Although there's been a fair amount of positive publicity about our business recently that might lead people to think we're well off financially. How about you, Caroline?"

She silently shakes her head no.

"Miss Bee, any light that you can shed on possible suspects or motives?" Bodine inquires.

She stammers and says, "Me? No! I'm just a woman working in a real estate office and going to nursing school part-time. I don't have a clue."

"And, you didn't see anyone unusual approach the house and assault you?"

"Why no, officer. It's like I said, I was playing with little Aurora in her crib, and the next thing I knew Mr. Engel was kneeling next to me, and I had a splitting headache."

The detective writes down her contact information, and asks Dr. Clodfelter if she's well enough to drive herself home. The doctor says she is.

"Miss Bee, here's my card. If you think of anything, anything at all, I want you to please call me, and we're gonna need you to stay in Putnam County until otherwise notified. Understand?"

"Yes, Detective, I understand." She gathers her purse and prepares to leave.

"Heather, what happened to the satchel you brought in with the diapers and cloths?"

"I don't know, ma'am, in all of the confusion I forgot all about it."

Detective Bodine gets a description of the carpetbag from her and tells her she's free to go.

"What now, Detective?" Delano asks again.

"Like I said, we wait for them to make contact again."

Caroline walks back into the nursery and clutches Aurora's baby blanket. She goes to a window and stares vacantly outside where she sees one of the police officers examining the ground near the grove of trees. A few minutes later the officer comes inside the house and speaks in low tones with Detective Bodine.

"What was that about, Detective?" Delano asks.

"My man says he found some footprints in the soft soil. They had a rather distinctive tread. I'd like to compare them with your shoes, Mr. Engel. If they don't match any of yours, it might give us a little bit of a lead."

Caroline goes into their closet and pulls out Delano's shoes.

"I also keep a pair of work boots in our mudroom. You'll want to check those too."

Bodine nods to his officer who takes a box filled with three pairs of Delano's shoes and heads down to the mudroom.

Caroline comes over and leans on her husband. "What're we going to do, Del? She means the world to us, and she's so small."

"I know, darling, just have faith. We'll get her back. The waiting is the hardest part now, but I promise you we'll get her back."

Thirty minutes later the telephone rings, and Detective Bodine stands near Delano to listen in on the call. He picks up the receiver.

Chapter 12

HEATHER BEE DRIVES her Nash automobile out of the Engels' driveway and turns east on Walnut Street toward Greencastle. She looks in her rearview mirror at her disheveled hair, then swerves to miss a pothole in the dirt road. She turns north on Indiana Street and drives slowly past the courthouse square. She glances quickly at the real estate office and doesn't see Rice Foxx's auto parked in front.

Heather continues heading north on State Route 231 toward the Putnam County fairgrounds and turns right on a little used road which is soggy from a recent flooding of Big Walnut Creek.

"No wonder Rice hasn't been able to sell this property. Who'd buy a shabby house whose basement gets flooded after every heavy rainfall?"

She approaches an old wooden frame house and pulls behind it and parks next to Rice's car. She looks in the mirror again at her hair and tries to shape it a bit. She winces as she brushes against the place where she'd been hit in the Engels' nursery. "For pity sakes, what I do for that man!"

She gets out of the Nash and enters the back door of the rundown house. "Where's the baby?" she hurls at Rice.

"In the living room. She's fine."

Heather slaps Rice hard across the face. "And, that's what you get for hitting me so hard, you big lummox!"

"Sorry, but I had to make it look convincing."

"Yeah, well, it felt pretty damn convincing too." She goes to slap him again, but he deflects her hand. She turns and goes into the living room to check on Aurora. "Ah, there you are, my sweet little one. Your Auntie Heather is here for you."

"Where'd you put her diapers and baby food, Rice?"

"It's there on the table. She's been crying a bunch, and I thought I'd just wait for you to get here and take care of her."

Heather gently picks Aurora up and sits on a tattered sofa. She places the infant on her lap and coos at her as she spoon feeds her creamed peas and carrots.

"She smells!" Rice laments.

"Well, you'd smell too if someone snatched you and stuffed you in a carpetbag." Once she's fed, Heather cleans the child up and changes her diaper. "Oh, you're such a love! And you, Rice Foxx, are a pain in the ass."

He dismisses the insult. "I've got to make another telephone call." He retreats to the kitchen, and Heather listens as he muffles his voice.

———

"Yes, this is Engel," Delano says into the receiver.

"Okay, Engel, this is how it's gonna be if you want your kid back with all of her body parts in place. I need you to pull together $100,000. You've got twenty-four hours to do that. I'll call you tomorrow and tell you where I want you to leave it, understand?!"

"But, I don't have $100,000," Delano pleads.

"Not my problem. You figure it out. Twenty-four hours…and no cops! Got it. If I see one blue uniform, your kid is history!" Rice hangs up.

Delano stares at the telephone receiver. Anger and fear well up inside of him.

"You realize that if you pay this jerk, it doesn't guarantee you'll get your child back," Detective Bodine advises.

Delano hugs Caroline and replies, "Well, I don't see where we have much choice." He immediately places a phone call to Mr. Zyer in Chicago. "Dave, we have a problem, and I need your help." He proceeds to tell Mr. Zyer about the kidnapping and the ransom demand.

"I'll take care of it, Delano. I'll contact your local bank and tell them I'll wire the money to them posthaste and ask that they advance the money to you in the meantime. I'm so sorry. Please tell Caroline that I'll do everything I can from my end." They hang up.

"Well, that part's done," he says to Caroline and the detective. "Now, we just wait twenty-four hours, I guess."

Detective Bodine asks them a few more questions and wonders, "Mrs. Engel, you said that you locked the front door when you went to meet Mr. Engel in the carriage house. I still don't know how the kidnapper got in unless someone unlocked the door for him. How well do you know Heather Bee?"

"Heather has been with us ever since Aurora was born. She's been like a member of the family. You don't honestly suspect her, do you?"

The detective shrugs. "$100,000 is a lot of dough. People have done worse things for a lot less."

"But, how do you explain the knot on her head, Detective? She was unconscious when we entered the nursery."

Again, the detective shrugs. "In my business, we consider all possibilities, Mrs. Engel. I think we've done as much as we can for now. I'll be back tomorrow in time for the next phone call. I'm leaving two officers here to watch your home. If anything happens, they can radio me, okay? Try to get some rest. You're gonna need it." He exits the house, and the Engels look out the nursery's window and see him giving instructions to his officers.

"Oh, Del, I'm just heartsick about this."

"I know, sweetheart, me too. Let's try to get some sleep. We've got to stay strong now."

The despondent couple wash up and climb into their large brass bed. They hold each other tenderly bathed in a glowing moonlight streaming through their bedroom window. They're about to fall asleep when they hear a rustling sound like wind rushing through the house…"Come, come…."

Caroline nudges Delano. "Did you hear that?"

"Yes, I did. I was hoping that it was just my mind playing tricks with me. Being as busy as we've both been of late, I'd almost forgotten about the Tamberg book." He turns toward Caroline and sees that she's already slipped out of bed and is putting her robe on.

"C'mon, Del, if that damn book can shed some light on Aurora's kidnapper, I want to know it."

Delano grumbles and climbs out of bed too. He puts on his robe and slippers, and the two exhausted parents leave their warm bed behind and ascend the stairs to the attic. Caroline leads the way into the cedar closet and presses the knot on the paneling. The door opens slightly and Delano pulls it fully open. There, aglow in yellow moonlight the large book rests upon the writing surface of the rolltop desk. It's open and its pages appear blank. They approach the book and stare at it in silence, waiting for some sort of revelation.

"Okay, oh wise book of the Tambergs," Delano mutters sarcastically. "You've written that you're here for us if we need you. Well, we definitely need you now."

There is silence and the Engels look at each other in confused frustration. They turn to leave and hear a flutter of pages, then words begin to appear where there was nothing a moment before.

Your child is safe for now, but I've foretold you that there would be turmoil.

Caroline beseeches, "Do you know where our Aurora is? Can you help us get her back safely?"

The future is never a sure thing. I can only see so far into the realm of the unseen, But she was taken by greedy people who are known to you. Follow the instructions given to you, but remember Res non semper videntur... Things are not always as they seem.

"That's it?! That's the best you can tell us?" Delano asks stridently, but no more words appear in the book.

After waiting a few moments longer, Caroline and Delano close the door to the hidden room and return to their bed.

"Big damn help that stupid book is. It said it would be there for us. Dumbass book!" They lie silently side by side and somehow after staring at the dark ceiling for a long time, they finally manage to drift off to sleep.

Chapter 13

A SOFT DAWN SUNLIGHT rises through the Engels' grove of trees and shimmers into their bedroom window. It slowly wends across the walls and shines its countenance on Caroline's face. Her eyes flutter open from the encroaching brightness, and she rushes out of bed into the nursery, hoping to find Aurora safely sleeping in her crib. Alas, her hope is a foregone fantasy as the crib lays void of her precious child. Crestfallen, she stares out of the nursery window at the rosy-fingered dawn and softly weeps, "Oh, Aurora...."

A few moments later Delano is standing beside his heartbroken wife, and they both stare vacantly at the beginning of a new day, one that will either bring them joyous relief or a crushing blow to their spirits.

"C'mon, darling, let's get dressed and go to the kitchen for some coffee and breakfast. We need to be ready when Detective Bodine returns, and I imagine the police officers outside might appreciate some coffee as well. Caroline nods her agreement, and they turn away from the nursery window.

While Caroline finishes preparing their break-fast, Delano takes two steaming mugs of black coffee to the uniformed officers outside.

"You men must be bushed after being on duty all night. Hopefully, this will help."

"Thank you, Mr. Engel, our old thermos bottles only keep our Java warm for so long. Appreciate it!"

"So, quiet night, I take it," Delano offers.

"Yeah, pretty quiet," the other officer states, "but, I'll tell ya, you've got some very unusual sounds around your property. For the life of us, we couldn't figure out where they were coming from, but it had to be from wind in the trees, right, Kissinger?"

"Dunno, remember, we first thought the sounds were coming from the house, but that made no sense. At one point the wind sounded like a voice speaking in low whispers. It was weird. And, we saw a bright light shining out of that window up in your roof tower. Figured you couldn't sleep and went up there for something, but aside from that it was a fairly uneventful night."

"Hmm, yeah, we heard it too," Delano replies without giving any details about the Tamberg book. "That is weird. Have you heard from Detective Bodine yet today?"

"Yeah, he radioed a few minutes ago and said he'd be out here around 9:00 AM with our relief officers."

The three of them chat for a few moments longer and then Delano returns to the kitchen to join Caroline.

Right on time Detective Bodine drives his car into the Engels' driveway and is followed by another police vehicle carrying two new officers. They exit their vehicles, and the cops exchange information about the previous uneventful night, and Officer Kissinger and his partner depart.

"Good morning, Mr. and Mrs. Engel, I presume that you haven't heard anything further from the kidnapper. I hope you managed to get some sleep."

"No, we haven't heard back from the kidnapper yet," Delano replies, "And no, we didn't get much sleep, Detective," Caroline adds.

"I've been wondering about possible suspects, you know, trying to narrow our search, and I keep thinking about how the kidnapper was able to enter your locked front door and manage to get upstairs into the nursery. There's no apparent damage to the door, and I believe Heather Bee would've heard something if there was a break-in."

"I know for certain that I locked the door before I met Delano in the carriage house," Caroline states.

"I understand, Mrs. Engel, that's what's got me puzzled. Either the perpetrator was intentionally let inside by your sitter who was then knocked unconscious, or the perp found a key on the porch somewhere and unlocked the door himself which I find rather unlikely. I attempted to telephone Miss

Bee before driving here, but she didn't answer her phone."

"Well, we do keep a spare key hidden by the stone angel sculpture in the garden," Delano offers, "but I checked on it after you left yesterday, and it's still there. I seriously doubt a kidnapper would've returned it to its hiding place once the front door was unlocked."

"I agree, Mr. Engel, and that's why I've just asked the sheriff to try to locate Heather Bee and bring her in for more questioning."

A few minutes later the telephone rings, and Delano grabs the receiver on the second ring with the detective listening nearby.

"Excellent, good, thank you," Delano says to the caller and then hangs up. "It was the bank. They've got the $100,000 ready, and it'll be delivered here shortly."

Thirty minutes later an unmarked van pulls into the yard, and the officers outside speak with the driver, then bring in a large case filled with one hundred dollar bills. "Now, we wait," Bodine says calmly.

An hour goes by, then two hours, and just when everyone is wondering if the exchange is going to occur, the telephone rings. Again, Delano answers the phone on the second ring.

"Yes, this is Delano Engel."

"You got the dough?" the muffled voice asks.

"Yes, I have what you asked for. Is Aurora safe?"

"Yeah, your kid's safe, and I hope you want to keep her that way."

"When can we meet?"

"First things first, Engel. I told you no cops, and you've got 'em crawling all over your place."

"But…." Delano begins.

"No buts, Engel, now, you either get serious, and I mean real serious, about getting your kid back, or I walk away, and you never see her again. Do I make myself clear?"

Delano hears a baby crying in the background. "Just please don't hurt her. I'll do as you ask. I promise."

"All right, then. You load up your car with the money and drive over to Round Barn Road east of town. You know where I'm talking about?"

"Yes, I know where it is."

"There's an old church about a mile down the road near a railroad overpass. The church is empty this time of day. You drive to it alone, understand?"

"What do you want me to do when I get there?"

"Go around to the back of the church, and you'll see instructions pinned to the rear door. If I see any cops, you'll never see that kid again. You've got twenty minutes to get there." The kidnapper hangs up.

Delano and Detective Bodine stare at each other and tell Caroline what the muffled voice said.

"Do you think he'll act in good faith?" Caroline beseeches the detective.

Bodine shrugs, "Hopefully. C'mon, let's get the money into your car."

"There's something I want you and Caroline to do, Detective."

"Oh, what's that?"

Instead of answering him immediately, Delano picks up the phone and calls Brian at the Putnam County airport. Brian answers on the third ring.

"Brian, it's Delano, we have an emergency, and I don't have much time to explain. I need you to fuel up the Jenny and have her on the runway ready for takeoff. A police detective will be with Caroline, and they'll need to be able to take off immediately. I wish I had time to explain more, but it's a matter of life and death. They'll be there in about fifteen minutes, okay?"

"I hear you, Del. Jenny's already fueled up. I'll push her out onto the runway, and she'll be ready to fly as soon as Caroline and the detective get here." Brian begins to say more, but Delano has already hung up.

"Caroline, honey, I don't know if this will help, but I want you and Bodine to be in the air circling over that church at a decent altitude so you won't draw attention to yourself, but close enough that you can spot any vehicles. We need to know where that kidnapper is going after he gets the money. Do you think you can do that?"

"Yeah, I can do that, Del. Sure beats staying here fretting myself to death."

"That's my gal. I've gotta go. I'll meet you two back at the airfield once I've dropped the money off at the church and followed the kidnapper's instructions." Delano gives his wife a tight embrace, tells her he loves her, and bolts out the door.

Caroline and Detective Bodine immediately follow him out and climb into Bodine's vehicle. "Ever flown before, Detective?" she asks.

"Uh no," he replies very nervously.

"Not a problem!" she says confidently. "I have!"

Chapter 14

Some fifteen minutes later Delano cautiously steers his Ford Model T from Round Barn Road into the old church's empty parking lot. He comes to a stop in front of the church and takes the car out of gear. He tries to calm his breathing and looks anxiously in all directions to see if anyone's around. He waits a few moments longer to let the auto's engine cool down from his speedy traverse across town, then engages the gear, and slowly drives to the back of the church and parks next to the rear entrance. He waits briefly to see if anyone appears, then shuts off the engine and climbs out. He moves quickly to the church's rear door, and as the kidnapper had promised, he sees a note pinned to the door.

"Leave the money inside the church's sacristy, then immediately continue driving north on Round Barn Road for a half mile until you come to Crow's bridge spanning Big Walnut Creek. Under the bridge by the south pile you'll see a carpetbag with your daughter inside."

Elated at the prospect of rescuing Aurora, Delano feels a surge of adrenaline as he runs back to the car and lifts the heavy chest full of money out of the boot, then half carries, half drags it through the church door into the sacristy. He bolts back to the car, restarts the engine, and sprays dirt and gravel as he speeds out of the lot heading north for Crow's bridge.

"Please be there," he prays aloud. With his window down he hears the familiar droning sound of an aeroplane engine overhead. He spies a steel truss bridge about a half mile ahead and coaxes every bit of speed that he can out of the Ford's engine. A minute later he arrives at Big Walnut Creek, kills the engine, and dashes on foot for the underside of the bridge.

Caroline keeps a close eye on Jenny's gauges and her rookie passenger as the aeroplane rises into the sky. She smiles briefly as she sees Detective Bodine's knuckles turn white from tightly gripping the sides of his cockpit, but then she's all down to business as she flies Jenny in the direction of Round Barn Road. To his credit, Bodine manages to relax a bit as his professionalism kicks in. He soon spots the old round barn for which the road is named, and shortly thereafter he points to the old church. Caroline sees Delano's Tin Lizzie exit the church lot and head north toward the bridge over Big Walnut Creek. Then, Caroline puts Jenny into a wide circling pattern looking for the kidnapper to arrive to pick up the ransom money.

Within a few minutes the detective spots a nondescript automobile entering the church lot and driving to the rear. Caroline continues to circle at an altitude that ensures their anonymity but gives them a clear view of the action below. They see a lone figure exit his car and run inside the church. A minute later they see a man wrestling the ransom chest into his vehicle and speed away toward Albin Pond Road.

"Follow that car!" the detective shouts excitedly. "Don't lose him!"

Caroline maintains her current altitude, while Bodine uses the plane's recently installed Marconi radio to alert his officers on the ground that they've got eyes on the perpetrator.

"He's on Albin Pond Road heading in the direction of State Route 231 and the Monon railroad crossing. Discreetly head in that direction and await my orders."

A couple of minutes later the kidnapper's automobile turns onto a dirt road near the county fairgrounds and drives toward a secluded, ramshackle wooden frame farmhouse.

Bodine radios to his men: "He's turned onto an unmarked dirt road just before you get to the fairgrounds. It appears that there's only one road leading to an old house, but it's a heavily wooded area so I can't tell for sure. Put up a roadblock at the entrance to the road so he can't escape the way he came in. Once you're in position Mrs. Engel and I will fly back to the airfield and get my car. Do not, I repeat do not try to apprehend the kidnapper until I get there unless he tries to break through the road-block. I should be there in about twenty minutes."

Caroline circles the Jenny and watches as four police vehicles approach and block the entrance to the road. Then, she immediately turns the plane in the direction of the airfield and radios ahead to Brian to let him know they're on their way back.

———

Delano quickly eyes his surroundings to see if he's being watched, then carefully walks beneath the bridge to the creek's sandy bank. By the stone bridge abutment, he sees the carpetbag and dashes toward it. He sees movement inside and calls out, "Aurora, it's papa! I've come to take you home." A moment later he unzips the satchel, and his world gets torn asunder as a large tabby cat leaps from the bag and hightails it for the nearby bushes. Aurora is nowhere to be found.

Delano is crestfallen. He's done everything that the kidnapper instructed, but to no avail. Now, their baby is still in the hands of a lying criminal, and he and Caroline are probably out $100,000. He grabs the carpetbag and runs back to his Model T thinking that maybe he still has time to retrieve the ransom. He guns the engine and speeds back to the rear of the old church. He leaps from the car and races through the rear door to the sacristy. His spirits are dashed twice within just a few minutes as he sees that the ransom chest has been taken. He slumps to the floor, stares at a crucifix mounted on the wall and weeps.

Ten minutes later Caroline sees Delano's Model T pull up to the aeroplane hangar, and she anxiously runs to greet him.

"Did you get her?! Is Aurora safe?!" From the expression on her husband's face, she immediately knows that the news is not good.

"The bastard screwed us, Caroline. Aurora wasn't there. Just some damn cat that he'd put inside the bag…and the money's gone."

She hugs her husband tightly, both heartbroken by the betrayal. "I swear to God, Caroline, we'll get our baby back safely. I promise you."

"I know, sweetheart, I know," she consoles.

"Where's Bodine, and what did you guys see from the air?"

"We saw a car enter the church lot very soon after you left for the bridge. A lone man ran inside the church and hauled out the ransom then drove down Albin Pond Road."

"Were you able to follow him? Did you see where he went?"

"Fortunately, we did. He drove to a secluded house near the fairgrounds. Detective Bodine radioed his officers, and they've set up a roadblock so the kidnapper can't escape the way he drove in. Bodine instructed his men to wait for him before trying to apprehend the kidnapper. He left here just a few minutes ago."

"C'mon, Caroline, let's drive over there. We need to be there for Aurora as soon as we can."

Delano shouts his thanks to Brian, and the couple climb into their car and speed away toward the fairgrounds. When they arrive Bodine is at the roadblock with a pair of binoculars inspecting the scene.

"What do you have, Detective?" Delano asks. "See any sign of the kidnapper or our baby?"

"Pretty quiet although we know they're in there. We're waiting for an ambulance to arrive just in case, then we'll move in. I promise we'll do everything possible to keep your baby safe."

Inside the old house Rice Foxx is an emotional mess, a combination of excitement at having snookered the cops and that rich guy, Delano Engel, plus being scared shitless knowing that he's public enemy number one for having snatched an infant. He sits at a folding table with his car keys and wallet next to an open glass of whiskey. Heather Bee sits on a threadbare sofa with little Aurora on her lap.

"What's next, Rice? I suppose you know our lives in good ol' Greencastle are history now."

"Yeah, but at least we've got a hundred grand to make a fresh start, and who knows, maybe we can get even more dough out of that Engel fella and his pretty little wife. For now, we just sit tight and wait for the sun to go down, then we try to sneak outta here. I transferred the money to your Nash in case someone recognized me driving here. We gotta be ready for a fast getaway. By the way, we got anything to eat? I'm starved from all of this excitement!"

Heather sets Aurora on the sofa and covers her with a blanket. She goes to the kitchen and opens a cabinet where they'd previously stored some crackers and peanut butter. Rice pours himself another glass of whiskey and stares giddily into space. "Yup, gonna make a fresh start, you and me."

In the blink of an eye, Heather wipes the grin off of Rice's face by smacking him hard in the head, once then twice, with an iron skillet. The real estate agent turned kidnapper slumps face first onto the table out cold. She checks to see if he's still breathing, which he is, then polishes off the remainder of whiskey in his glass. Heather collects all of the baby supplies and places them in a large sack and totes them out to her car, then double-checks to make certain the loot is stashed away in her trunk. She returns for Aurora and gently lifts the child into her arms and coos at her. "Let's go, sweetie, you and your new mommy are gonna make a fresh start just like good ol' Ricey Poo said."

A minute later Heather drives her car down a hidden grassy lane behind the house to the edge of a cow pasture and then off into the twilight.

After the ambulance arrives without flashing lights or siren, Bodine signals his men to surround the farmhouse and begin to close in. He instructs the Engels to hang back, but they're having none of it.

"We didn't go through all of this just to stay put, did we, Del?" and the Engels begin walking furtively toward the farmhouse. Bodine shrugs and follows after them.

Bodine radios all of his men to confirm that they're in position around the house, then he directs his men to break through the front and rear doors at the same time. A few moments later, the Engels hear loud crashes of wood as the cops burst in. They see a slumped-over figure at the table, but the rest of the house is empty. One of the officers steps outside onto the porch and signals to Detective Bodine that the premises are secure. Bodine and the Engels enter and are shocked when they see that their real estate agent, Rice Foxx, is alone and unconscious with no sign of the child or the ransom money anywhere.

For the Engels it's like all of the oxygen has been sucked out of the room.

Chapter 15

D ETECTIVE BODINE DIRECTS the medical personnel to attend to Rice Foxx while he clears the remainder of his men outside so he can have a better sense of the crime scene. Used cloth diapers and baby food containers are inside an old trash can which confirms to the Engels that their baby is still alive and being tended to.

Rice Foxx gradually returns to consciousness and is surprised and agitated by being in the hands of law enforcement officers.

"Who? What?" he stammers as he's placed in handcuffs. "But…"

"Where's the child?" Bodine hurls at the suspect. "Where is she, and who's got her?"

Delano grabs Rice by the shirt collar and prepares to deal out his own form of interrogation when the detective pushes him away. "We'll take care of this now, Mr. Engel. Why don't you and Mrs. Engel go outside for a few minutes so I can do my job?!"

Delano tries to lunge at Foxx again, but Caroline intercedes. "C'mon, Del, we've got to let the detective question this worm." They go outside on the porch.

"Okay, Mr. Foxx, let's take this from the top. Where's the child, and who's got her, and where did they go? Is Heather Bee your accomplice?"

"What child, officer? I have no idea what you're taking about. I was here looking at this house as a potential property to sell, and all of a sudden I wake up and you and your people are hovering over me."

"That's not going to cut it, Foxx, we know you kidnapped the Engels' child and got the ransom. This will go a lot easier for you if you just come clean now. We need to know where the girl is now, and if your employee, Miss Bee, has her. And, I promise you if anything happens to the child, we'll be adding a murder charge to kidnapping. At the very least you'll be locked away for the rest of your life."

Rice Foxx tries to get his wits about him and says, "I have no idea what you're taking about, Detective. I want a lawyer."

"Are you sure you want to stick to your story, Foxx? We have very credible witnesses that saw you pick up the ransom money at the church and drive here."

"Oh, and who might those witnesses be?" he challenges.

"Well, me for one and Mrs. Engel for another."

"I want a lawyer," Foxx repeats.

Detective Bodine asks the medical team if the suspect is stable enough for transport to the jail, and when they say yes, he roughly lifts Rice from his chair and shoves him into the arms of two other officers. "Get him the hell out of here and drag his ass to county lockup! We've got you cold, Foxx!"

Caroline and Delano glare at their former real estate agent as he's led away, then go inside to talk with Bodine.

"So, what do we do now, Detective? Aurora could be anywhere."

"I've got to believe that Miss Bee is Mr. Foxx's accomplice and that she's got your child. Any idea what kind of automobile she might be driving?"

"She always drives a Nash," Caroline replies, "but she may try to ditch that for something else, and if she's got the $100,000, it won't be hard for her to swap it for something else."

Bodine nods his agreement but radios to his dispatcher to put out a countywide APB, and to alert law enforcement in surrounding counties to be on the lookout for a Nash vehicle driven by a woman.

"What else can you do, Detective? What can Caroline and I do now? We can't just let this woman get away with our Aurora!"

"For now, we'll have to see what our officers turn up. If, in fact, it is Heather Bee who has Aurora, we'll find her. She won't make it out of Putnam County. As for the two of you, I want you to please return home and await word from me. I promise you that I'll call you as soon as I have anything to share."

Delano begins to protest, but Caroline convinces him that Bodine is correct. "There's nothing we can do now, Del, except wait for the police to do their work."

"Do you promise that you'll let us know the moment you learn anything, Detective?" Delano beseeches.

"I do. Please just go home now and try to get some rest, okay?"

Delano and Caroline reluctantly walk away from the farmhouse and return to their car parked by the roadblock. They get in and Delano drives them back toward town. They're both physically and emotionally numb with exhaustion. They return home in silence and sit still in the car. Caroline touches Delano's hand, and they both give each other a feeble smile of reassurance. "We'll get her back, Caroline. We'll get our baby back."

They exit the Model T and stare up at the starry sky shining its gem-like brilliance over their house. "Thank goodness you and Bodine were able to spot Foxx's movements from the air. At least we've got that bastard, and hopefully the detective will be able to get him to confess and say where Heather Bee might've gone."

"I still don't quite understand why Heather was unconscious in the nursery and how Foxx got into the house after I'd locked the front door. Or, why Foxx was unconscious in the farmhouse...unless these people just make a habit of whacking on each other."

"I imagine we'll eventually get answers to these questions, but for now, I'm totally bushed, sweetheart."

Delano glances skyward again as if looking for divine inspiration when he sees a soft golden glow coming from the small window in the roof tower. He draws Caroline's attention to it.

"I don't have the energy to deal with that damn Tamberg book right now. Maybe in the morning."

Heather Bee uses the cover of darkness as she drives out Manhattan Road to a sprawling property that she knows is currently vacant. Victoria and Linville Jefferson have traveled to Boston to visit their son's family and had hired the Big Walnut Real Estate

Company to look after their home during a month-long stay.

The main house is a grand white mansion sitting atop a hill overlooking their fields and the county road beyond. The gravel driveway is nearly a quarter mile long with mature pine trees and a pond on either side. Heather drives her Nash past the main house and pulls up to a lovely yellow carriage house that the Jeffersons had renovated into a guest quarters. Its remote location is perfect for Heather to conceal herself and little Aurora until things calm down. She pulls her car behind the carriage house to keep it hidden from unwanted eyes and then totes the child and her accoutrements into the house.

"Here we are, sweetie. We're gonna be snug as bugs in a rug! How's that sound?!"

Heather returns outside to the car and pops open the trunk revealing the chest of money. She flips the lid open and stuffs a wad of bills into her pocket. "Yessir! Snug as bugs in a rug!"

At the Putnam County jail Rice Foxx is led in irons into an interrogation room. His head still smarts from where Heather had whomped him with the iron skillet, and being locked up hasn't improved his mood much. Buster Bodine enters the room and sits opposite Foxx at a rough pine table.

"So, Mr. Foxx, I suppose you're finding your accommodations here in our little establishment to your liking," he remarks sarcastically.

Rice Foxx is not in the mood for jailhouse humor. "When do I get to call an attorney? I've been framed, you know."

"Oh, and who would be framing you, sir? And does that individual have the child?"

"I want to speak to my attorney."

"You'll be able to do that shortly, but I wanted to give you an opportunity to reconsider your story and perhaps win a free upgrade in our accommodations."

"Nice try, Detective, but it's like I told you, I was at that farmhouse inspecting it as a potential property to sell, and someone clobbered me from behind."

"Oh, and how do you explain the used diapers and baby food containers we found in the wastebasket?"

"I dunno. Could've been the homeowner. You know, some people just aren't very tidy these days."

"Uh huh," Bodine replies flatly. "Real shame you lost out on all of that money. Now, your partner's got it, and you've got nothing but a busted-up head and a long prison term facing you. Yeah, I bet you want to speak with an attorney now, but I doubt he'll be able to do you much good, what with me and Mrs. Engel seeing you pick up the money at the church and drive to that farmhouse. Nope, I reckon that the best attorney in the state couldn't get you out of this mess. So, why don't you just come clean and tell us about how you and Heather Bee hatched your kidnapping plan? You know, it's just a matter of time before we nab her and return the child to the Engels anyway, and gee, all of that money slipping through your hands."

Rice Foxx shifts nervously in his chair. "You're a real prick, you know that don't ya, Bodine?"

"Okay, Guard, the interrogation is over," the detective shouts through the door. "Come and get Mr. Foxx. He's entitled to one phone call to his attorney." Bodine stands up to leave.

"All right, it was Heather and me," Foxx confesses. The detective asks the guard to have a stenographer join them, and he sits down again at the table. A moment later they're joined by a matronly looking woman with a pad and pen.

"As you were saying, Mr. Foxx...."

Over the course of the next hour Rice Foxx explains how he'd originally met the Engels and helped them close on the purchase of their house. "Damn people have all the money in the world, and here Heather and I are working hard to make ends meet."

"Go on," Bodine prompts.

"So, it's like I said, they paid cash for this really nice house and have an aeroplane and their own company, and when Heather started working there to help them after the baby was born, we figured we'd bide our time and then snatch the kid for a large ransom. Worked pretty well too...until it didn't."

"So, how'd you gain entry to the house? Did Miss Bee let you in, as we suspected?"

"Naw, when the Engels bought the house, I encouraged them to have the old locks changed.

Delano was comfortable with me hiring a locksmith, and well, I had an extra set of door keys made that I just hung on to."

"Why was Miss Bee unconscious when the Engels returned to the nursery?"

"Well, I had to make it look like she wasn't involved, so I hit her in the head when she wasn't looking. She apparently wasn't very happy with me for that, and I guess that's why she, uh, returned the favor at the farmhouse."

"I reckon so," Bodine agrees. "And now for the $100,000 question, where's Miss Bee now, Foxx?"

"Damned if I know. That miserable excuse for a partner could be anywhere."

"So, you two never discussed a contingency plan in case your original scheme didn't work out?"

"Nope, we were just going to get the money and skedaddle out of the county. Start fresh someplace else. She kept talking about wanting to keep the Engel kid for herself. Seemed like she'd gotten rather fond of the little tyke from working over there. I figured maybe it wasn't a bad idea in case we wanted to get the Engels to sweeten the pot some more."

"So, you don't know where Heather and the child are, right?"

"Not a clue, Detective. So, when do you suppose I'll be able to get out of here on bail?"

"Uh, like never!" Bodine replies. "You do realize that kidnapping is a federal offense, don't you?"

"Uh, I wasn't sure because I've never done this before," Rice says sheepishly. "Besides, I'm cooperating with you now, aren't I?"

"You're a real prince, Foxx. Now, I encourage you to call an attorney, and if you can't retain one, the State of Indiana will be happy to provide one for you. Naturally, if you think of anything else that might help us safely rescue the Engel child and bring Heather Bee to justice, you might be able to spend the rest of your days in a comfier institution. Let me know if anything helpful jogs your memory. Guard!"

Chapter 16

D ELANO AWAKES SLOWLY the next morning, his mind in a bit of a daze, then his eyes shoot wide open as he fully recalls the frustration of their not finding Aurora at the farmhouse last evening. He sits at the side of the bed mentally resurrecting the details of leaving the ransom money only to have a big cat jump out of the carpetbag that was supposed to hold Aurora. Thank goodness Caroline and Bodine had followed Rice Foxx to the farmhouse from the air, but damn-it-to-hell for not getting their baby back. "Now what?!" he mutters aloud.

In a sleepy voice Caroline says, "Now we pray for some divine inspiration, sweetheart."

They both get out of bed and put on robes and walk into the nursery. They watch the sunlight reflect off the brightly colored mobile hanging over the crib. Caroline turns a little handle, and the mobile moves slowly and its music box plays a sweet metallic tune. She sighs and leads Delano away from the nursery and downstairs to the kitchen.

They putter around quietly as Caroline prepares coffee and Delano cooks up bacon and eggs in a skillet. He stares vacantly as breakfast sizzles and wonders if Detective Bodine was able to wrestle any helpful information out of that son of a bitch, Rice Foxx.

"C'mon, Del, let's have our breakfast on the patio. It's a pretty day, and maybe the sunlight will brighten our moods a bit."

Delano slides their breakfasts onto plates, and Caroline holds the door open for him while balancing two coffee mugs. They sit at the patio table watching songbirds flit from branch to branch, chirping in the warm sunlight. The stone statue of the angel stands silently in the nearby garden plot, a reminder of their missing little one.

"If we believe we're gonna get any divine inspiration from the garden angel, I think we'll be sorely disappointed, love," Delano offers somberly. He shifts his gaze to the treetops and follows a pair of mourning doves as they land on the roof tower. He recalls seeing the soft golden light coming from the little window when they returned home last night and sighs, "Maybe the Tamberg book can help guide us after all, Caroline. I'm not sure that we have anything to lose, do you?"

"No, I suppose not, Del. I fear we're running out of options…and time. Let's finish up here and see what kind of, uh, magic the sum knowledge of the Tamberg Dynasty can conjure up for us."

They clean up the kitchen and get dressed. Delano places a telephone call to Detective Bodine asking for any news.

"I was just about to call you since I knew that you and the missus would be eager for any information that we learned from Foxx."

"And?" Delano prompts.

"And, the good news is that he's confessed to the kidnapping, but the bad news is that he doesn't have a clue where Heather Bee and Aurora are."

"We were afraid of that. What're your plans now, Detective?"

"We have our officers plus the Indiana State Police patrolling virtually every road in Putnam County and roads entering into contiguous counties. My guess is that Miss Bee is holed up somewhere in our county waiting for the dust to settle a bit. I'll continue to lean on Foxx to see if I can rattle any more information out of him. I promise to keep you posted as I learn anything."

"Thanks, Detective. We appreciate everything you're doing."

They hang up, and Delano asks Caroline if she's ready to head up to the attic. They reach the large room at the top of the stairs and hear a whirling sound of wind similar to what they've heard previously. They look at each other knowingly.

"I guess our presence is requested," Caroline says of the sentient book. "Shall we oblige our green, paginated friend?"

They enter the cedar closet by the tower room, and Caroline presses the knot in the cedar paneling. As before, the paneling opens slightly and Delano pulls the panel open revealing the hidden room with the rolltop desk and the large old book resting on its writing surface. Sunlight from the little window illuminates the interior space. They approach the book and wait.

A few moments pass and Caroline speaks in a soft respectful voice, "If we ever needed your help, now is the time. We miss our daughter so much and pray that she's safe and that we can bring her home very soon."

The Book of the Tambergs lies silent, and the Engels grow anxious with each moment that passes, then its pages begin to flutter and words in an ancient-looking script begin to scroll across the heretofore blank page.

I sense the pain that you feel,
and I am sorry for the turmoil
that you have to endure.

Humankind can be very
petty and cruel...

"Can you please help us?" Caroline beseeches. "The authorities are doing all that they can, and honestly, we don't know what more we can do. Our child means the world to us, and life without her would be a fate worse than death to my husband and me."

Yes, humankind can be most unkind.
I have told you that you have been
chosen to protect my secrets,
and in return I am here to guide you.
I shall help you as I am able.

"Can you please tell us where our dear Aurora is?" Delano begs. "Can you tell us where to look?" The book's pages flutter again and reveal another blank page. Then, words in a black script begin to flow from a realm unseen across the empty space.

I cannot tell you an exact location,
But I can point you in a direction
To reach your destination.

"Yes, Yes! Whatever you can do. Please, yes!" Moments pass that feel like an eternity, and the green tome's pages flutter anew.

Seek a place where houses exist on paper,
Where owners come and go.
There you shall learn of a place
to find your daughter,
Then take flight to bring her home.

The Engels stare at each other, hoping that the other has a clue what the Tamberg book's words mean. Both shrug in frustration.

"We don't understand what that means. Can you please be more specific?" But, the book remains silent, and Caroline and Delano are left scratching their heads for greater clarity.

"Please, what does that mean? We need your guidance, please!"

That is all that I have the power to share.
I believe you possess the skills
to find your way...

The words from the book cease to flow, and Caroline and Delano are left standing in a small room with a rolltop desk, an old green book, and an enigma that tries their souls. Several painstakingly long moments later they exit the hidden room, close the cedar panel, and walk toward the attic steps leading downstairs. They return to the nursery and stare out the curved glass windows.

"I have no idea what that means, Del. I feel like we're no closer to finding Aurora than we were before we visited the book."

"It is, indeed, a mystery, but let's try to take it one step at a time, sweetheart. I prefer to think that the book would only write those words if it sensed that we could truly divine their meaning."

Caroline repeats the first two sentences from memory: *"Seek a place where houses exist on paper, where owners come and go."*

Just then the telephone rings, and Caroline answers it. "It's Bodine," she whispers to Delano. "Any news, Detective?"

"Maybe," he replies. "Foxx is pretty angry with how Heather Bee hung him out to dry with us. Says she's the one who concocted this scheme to kidnap Aurora, etc. etc."

"Well, it's kind of a moot point now isn't it, Detective, since they were both willing participants?"

"No question, Mrs. Engel. He's going away for a long time. He did say something that makes sense though. Said Heather was the one who kept a lot of the office records. In all of the drama, we really haven't done an adequate search of the Big Walnut Real Estate office. Why don't you and Mr. Engel meet me over there? Maybe we can come up with something."

"Sounds like a good idea. How about in thirty minutes?"

They hang up, and the Engels finish doing a few things around the house, then hop into the Model

T. "I'm still trying to figure out what the Tamberg book meant about houses existing on paper and where owners come and go. Seems to me that a real estate office is as good as any place to start."

When they pull up to the courthouse square, they park between a horse-drawn wagon and Bodine's vehicle. The bell on the office door tinkles as they enter, and the detective looks up from Rice Foxx's desk to greet them.

"G'morning, hope you folks were able to get some sleep last night."

"Some, but not much," Delano replies. "It's a relief to have Foxx locked up, but I doubt we'll ever be able to sleep peacefully until we get Aurora back safely."

"Find anything in his desk, Detective?" Caroline queries.

"Not yet. There's a lot of paperwork to go through. Why don't you two go through Miss Bee's desk since she probably handled a lot of the clerical materials."

Caroline sits in Heather's chair and begins going through her drawers while Delano begins looking through the copious amount of paperwork on the desk's top. "Gee, where's a sentient book when you need one?" he whispers to Caroline.

After about fifteen minutes, Buster Bodine says, "I think I've gone through his files about as well as I can. Really don't see much here other than normal business transactions."

Caroline finishes going through Heather's drawers, then turns her attention to her desk calendar. A notation from a few days earlier says to begin daily care at Jeffersons' home: *pick up mail, water house plants, feed cat. They return in four weeks from Boston.*

Caroline originally dismisses the note as just another duty that a real estate firm might handle, especially for a well-off client. But then, she recalls the book's message and thinks that a real estate office is definitely a place where houses exist on paper and where homeowners come and go. She sits upright in her chair and says aloud, "I think I might have something."

Delano and Bodine join her at Heather's desk and see the reference to the Jeffersons' home on Manhattan Road. They agree that a large property whose owners are gone for a month could be a perfect location for Heather to hide.

"Good work, Mrs. Engel. Definitely worth a look." Bodine picks up the phone and dials police headquarters.

Chapter 17

HEATHER WRAPS AURORA in a blanket and walks outside with her to the Nash. She pulls a stroller out of the trunk and then checks to see that all the doors are locked to protect the chest of cash.

"Here you go, sweetie, we're just gonna take a little walk up to the big house to see what kind of food and clothing we can, uh, borrow. We've got to make sure you have something yummy and wholesome to eat, don't we?"

The big house is only about a hundred yards away, but the gravel driveway presents a bit of a challenge for the stroller's small wheels. Heather ends up dragging the stroller the final few yards rather than trying to push it. She takes a door key from her pocket that the Jeffersons had left at the real estate office and inserts it into the lock.

"Ah, there we go," Heather says as she unlocks the backdoor and brings both Aurora and the stroller inside. The interior of the Jeffersons' home is spacious and grand. It has an enormous kitchen with a large pantry and a walk-in freezer. The Jeffersons often have their children and grandchildren visit them, so it doesn't take long for Heather to find a good supply of baby food for Aurora and other canned items.

"I think we've hit the motherlode, sweetie! We could stay here for a long time if we needed to, but I think it's best if we just disappear in a day or so. Would you like to go to Florida? I hear tell it's right pretty down there, and I'm sick of all the snow we get anyway, aren't you?" Aurora just coos and then all of a sudden starts to cry.

"Oh, is someone hungry or do you need your diaper changed?" Heather feels down below and sees that it's the latter. Your new mommy's gonna need to pick up some more cloth diapers real soon. Would you like to take a drive over to that little grocery store in Reelsville after eating your pureed vegetables and a nap? That would be fun, wouldn't it?"

Heather feeds and changes the little girl and fixes herself some fried SPAM® for lunch. I could use a little nap too, darlin', why don't we curl up here on this large sofa and catch a few winks. How's that sound?"

About thirty minutes later Heather is aroused from her nap by the sound of someone knocking on the backdoor. She wipes the vestiges of sleep from her eyes and cautiously peers around a corner through an adjacent window. She notices a man in workman's clothes waiting and goes to see who it is. She opens the door a crack.

"Yes?" she asks cautiously, "Who is it?"

"I'm Perry Custer, ma'am. I mow the Jeffersons' lawn for them. I was hoping to get paid for my mowing a couple of days ago."

"Uh, yes, I recall Mrs. Jefferson saying that you'd be here on a weekly basis. How much do they owe you?"

"Well, given the size of the yard, and my doing the mowing and edging, we'd agree upon twenty dollars each week."

"Okay," Heather says. "Let's do this, I'll give you forty, so now you're paid in advance for next week too. How's that, Mr. Custer?"

"That would be swell, ma'am. I appreciate it. The Jeffersons always did take good care of me."

Custer begins to ask who she is, but Heather has already slipped two twenty-dollar bills through the door and said goodbye.

"Uh, thanks again, ma'am," he says through the closed door and steps away.

Heather returns to the sofa and sees Aurora's bright eyes looking up at her. "Hello, sweet girl, did someone have a good nap?" Aurora kicks her feet and giggles cheerfully.

Heather returns to the backdoor to see if Mr. Custer is still around. She watches him drive his pickup truck down the driveway and turn into the cornfield fronting along the county road. She sees him get out of the truck with a large yard tool and walk over to a nearby bass pond.

"Okay, Miss Aurora, now's probably as good a time as any to drive to the grocery in Reelsville. Let me get you situated in the stroller, and we'll go back down to my car."

Five minutes later the two of them are in the Nash and heading quietly down the driveway. As they turn west on Manhattan Road, they see Mr. Custer's truck, and the yard man is using a scythe to clear some tall cattails near the Jeffersons' pond. They promptly exit the property unseen.

———

"Okay, men," Detective Bodine says to four of his officers, "We're following a hunch that the kidnapper and the child may be holed up at the Jefferson property on Manhattan Road. Mr. and Mrs. Engel will ride with me. Edberg, Wurster, Tweedie, and Hazel, you guys follow behind us. We're going in quietly. We don't know for sure if the suspect or any accomplice is there, but if so, we don't want to spook anyone, understand? Don't want to risk the child getting harmed."

The officers nod their understanding, and the Engels get very nervous as they see two of the officers load shotgun shells into their twelve-gauge Winchesters. They get into the two vehicles and head west through Limedale toward the Jefferson property.

Several minutes later they arrive near the Jefferson property and slow their approach to the driveway. They come to a halt to survey their surroundings, and Bodine orders Officers Tweedie and Wurster to guard the entrance while Officers Edberg and Hazel begin moving forward. They immediately come to a stop, though, when they see the yardman, Perry Custer, emerge from tall cattails. He's carrying the scythe and is surprised to see police officers all of a sudden train their weapons on him.

"Whoa!" he wails. "Easy with the heavy artillery. I'm just the yardman doing what the Jeffersons hired me to do."

"Turn around," Officer Edberg shouts. 'And, drop the scythe!"

Custer instantly does as he's commanded. "What's this all about? I'm just doing my job."

"Turn around and kneel on the ground with your hands raised high."

Custer begins to protest, and the officer shouts, "Do it now!"

Custer does it now, and Officer Hazel dashes forward and handcuffs the hapless yardman's hands behind his back.

"Who else is here?" Bodine queries Custer.

"I saw a woman up at the house about thirty minutes ago. I wanted to see about getting paid. I didn't know if anyone would be home, and this lady answered the door and paid me for two weeks. That's it. I swear that's all I know."

Officer Edberg leads Custer over to the officers guarding the driveway entrance and sits him on the ground and rejoins Bodine and Hazel. "Let's roll!" the detective says. "Edberg and Hazel, you guys search the main house, and the Engels and I'll take that carriage house." Ten minutes later the officers emerge having cleared both properties.

"No one's around, but we found more baby food containers and soiled diapers at both places. I think we must've just missed them," Bodine reports.

Caroline and Delano are frustrated beyond words. "Damn it, we can't seem to catch a break. They could be anywhere again, couldn't they?" Delano laments.

"Yes, they could, but the good news is that we know for sure that they were here, so they apparently haven't left Putnam County. My guess is that they'll be heading back this way, but Heather Bee holds all the cards at this point. I'll leave a couple of officers here to stake out the property in case she does return."

"And us?" Caroline asks. "What do you want us to do? It's the not-knowing that's really unsettling to us."

"I understand," Bodine replies. "Me, too, but we've got all of the roads pretty well staked out. Someone's gonna spot them. In the meantime I suggest that you take my car and return home. I want to question this Custer fella a little more, but I doubt that he knows much else. I promise you I'll be in touch the moment I know anything further. Here's a radio so we can stay in touch."

Caroline and Delano are very reluctant to leave but see little point in staying and get in Bodine's vehicle and head for home.

"I'm so scared and tired, Del, I just want our baby back."

"I know, honey. Bodine's proven he's committed to that...and maybe the Tamberg book has some more ideas."

Caroline looks expectantly at her husband. "Wouldn't hurt trying."

Heather Bee drives her Nash to Tavia's grocery store in the little village of Reelsville and locks Aurora inside while she runs in to buy food and supplies. Ten minutes later she emerges with sacks filled with cloth diapers, soap, more baby food, and a variety of food items for herself. She pulls into a gas station next door, fills the tank, and buys a road map.

"Okay, sweet thing," she says to Aurora as she enters the car. "We're good to go! Let's head back to the Jeffersons and lie low for the night, then skedaddle for sunny Florida."

She drives back the way she'd come and arrives at a rise in the road with the Jeffersons' property in view. Instinctively, she comes to a stop under a canopy of trees to check out the surroundings. That's when she spots people at the entrance to the driveway with Perry Custer sitting on the ground nearby.

"Damn it! Cops! Pardon my French," she says to Aurora. "Looks like a change of plans is in order. Stick with me, kiddo. I have a thought." She turns the Nash around and drives away.

Chapter 18

HEATHER DRIVES CAREFULLY along the back roads of western Putnam County avoiding as much traffic as possible. She passes the Boone-Hutcheson cemetery looming high on a hill and cruises through the Houck covered bridge as it spans Big Walnut Creek. After several more miles she finally arrives at the limestone quarry just west of Greencastle. The sun is getting lower in the sky now, and she watches the last exhausted crews of men leave for the day, dusty from having dragged and cut large rough blocks of stone into usable construction sizes.

From her days working in the real estate office with Rice Foxx, she's very familiar with many of the local properties and their various buildings. Long before the quarry was used as a quarry, it served as a religious retreat center, and a few of the original buildings are still standing. One such site is a modest spiritual alcove, literally carved out of the side of a limestone wall. It has a stout wooden door, a table and chair, and two old folding cots inside, with a sweet brook providing fresh water just outside. Heather had recalled playing here with friends, and the occasional boyfriend, during her school years, and it's here that she brings Aurora. She hides the Nash and brings the child and enough provisions inside, then lights a devotional candle, and they settle in for what she plans will be one last night in Greencastle, Indiana.

Delano and Caroline arrive home with the weight of the world on their shoulders. They know that with each hour that passes, and with each rescue attempt that's thwarted, the real possibility grows that they may never see their adorable child again.

They stand outside of the detective's car looking around their yard. The red carriage house where they'd made love just a day or so ago is a bittersweet memory to them since that's where they were when Aurora was kidnapped. They walk toward the house and see dew forming on the grass and arrive at the stone garden statue of the angel. Dewdrops fall along its bowed head looking like tears as they drip upon its cheek. Caroline leans against Delano as they look up and see pale golden moonlight reflecting off the small window in the roof tower, and he sees tears cascading down his heartbroken wife's face as well.

"C'mon, honey," he says softly. "Let's head inside and go visit our, uh, friend in the attic, shall we?"

Caroline takes his hand and leads him onto the porch and through the door with the name Wright and two doves immortalized in stained glass above.

"I don't know, Del, I'm awfully tired right now. Can we please put this off until morning? I just want to grab a quick bite to eat and hit the sack. Is that okay?"

"Sure," he whispers. "I'm pretty tired too." While Caroline is preparing a simple dinner, he radios Detective Bodine to see if there's anything to report.

"No, Mr. Engel, it's all quiet here. We let Perry Custer go, and I'm keeping Officers Wurster and Tweedie here overnight in case Heather Bee returns. I'm on my way back to Greencastle now. Officer Edberg's gonna drop me off briefly at your house so I can get my car, but I won't bother you and the missus. We'll talk in the morning."

They end their call, and Delano and Caroline sit at their dining table quietly eating their meal.

"I still can't believe that Heather and Rice Foxx kidnapped our child. We were good to them. We gave them business. We trusted her in our home with our baby. I just don't understand how people can behave that way."

"I know, honey, and you're right. I've never spoken with you much about the horrors of war I witnessed in France. Hell, I don't ever want to think about it again, and I sure don't like the thought of describing the unimaginable things I saw to you. But, if there's one thing I've learned it's that people can, and sometimes will, behave with inexplicable ugliness. The war forever changed the way I view the world, and it's only having you, and Aurora, and our dream of building a future together that repels the devils that I've known. I know I keep saying this, but I believe in my heart we'll get Aurora back safely, and that Foxx and Heather will pay dearly for their crimes."

They finish their meal, clean up the kitchen, and head for bed.

Upstairs, they put their belongings away and climb into bed. They lie very close and both stare at the ceiling. Candlelight from Caroline's bed stand casts mesmerizing shadows on the white plaster. A gentle breeze from an open window makes the candle flame shimmy, and the script-like shadows remind Delano of Ex Libris Tamberg, from the Library of Tamberg.

Caroline blows the candle out and bids sweet dreams to her husband. They hold hands together until she falls asleep. Despite feeling exhausted Delano can't get the thought of the sentient book out of his mind. He needs guidance now because otherwise they're all flying blind. He waits a few minutes more and listens as Caroline's breathing indicates she's deeply asleep. He doesn't want to disturb her. He then moves his blanket away and steps onto the floor and into his slippers and robe.

He lights another candle at the foot of the attic stairs and begins climbing the fifteen steps. He pauses halfway up wondering if the book can really provide the guidance it states it can.

"I sure hope so because time's running out," he whispers softly to himself, then continues his ascent.

He enters the cedar closet and walks to the rear panel and presses the knot. The door panel opens slightly, and he grips it and slides it fully open. Even with his candlelight the room before him appears dim and lifeless gray. He steps across the threshold and instantly the room bearing the rolltop desk and large book is bathed in a heartening glow. He approaches the Book of Tamberg, looking very much like a weary pilgrim in his cotton robe and well-worn slippers. He closes his eyes, and reverently says, "Help us, please."

At first the great book lies silent. A soft, shimmering gold aura radiates from the blank white pages. A moment later the aura grows tenfold in intensity and black script begins to appear on the page.

Yes, help indeed. There is much at risk.

Delano awaits a further reply and is frustrated by how demurely the book is responding to his plea. And then...

They are near, your child and the woman,
But it's not safe to attempt
to find them at night.
There are steep cliffs and areas
filled with deep water.
At first light, visit with me again.

Delano is very reluctant to leave but follows the book's instructions and descends the stairs. As he ponders the book's words, Delano can only think of one place nearby that has the kind of geology the book described. The limestone quarry.

"The book is right. The quarry is far too dangerous a place to venture at night. Tomorrow, at first light, is a new day."

Delano quietly disrobes and steps out of his slippers and into their bed. A few moments later he's asleep.

The next morning Delano wakes up before the first rays of sunlight pierce their window blinds. He gently touches Caroline's shoulder and urges her to wake up. Her eyes flutter open and she yawns.

"We need to get moving, Caroline."

"What, of course, where?" she asks still fighting off the cobwebs of sleep. "Delano, what time is it?"

He proceeds to tell her about visiting the book after she fell asleep last night.

"What did it say?"

"That Aurora is nearby, but that the location was not safe at night. It asked for us to revisit it at first light."

Caroline looks out the window and sees the sun barely rising through the trees. She's fully alert now and jumps out of bed into her robe and slippers. "First, I gotta pee, then let's go up!"

The anxious couple climb the stairs to the attic and enter the hidden room through the cedar door panel. Sunlight is just breaking into the room and falling on the Tamberg book. They approach the sentient book, and Caroline lightly touches a blank page. When she removes her fingers, the pages begin to flutter and the tome emits a radiant glow, then words begin to scroll across its surface.

Your child is safe, but soon
may be very far away.
You must be prepared to take flight
Lest you risk never seeing her again.

Caroline gasps, and Delano asks, "Is she in the quarry? Can we bring her home?"

Yes...and yes
But her kidnapper is sly
and feels emboldened.

You must act quickly.

"The quarry is a large place. Can you tell us where to look?"

Long ago it was a place of
spiritual reflection,
But now it's tainted by this transgression.
Seek and you may all be free.

Caroline asks the Tamberg book for more guidance, but no more words appear, and the book's radiance dissolves into thin air.

"C'mon, Caroline, we've got to get moving. I'll radio Bodine and have him meet us at the entrance to the quarry and establish a perimeter with his officers in case there's more than one access road."

"Why the quarry?" the detective asks on the radio.

"Let's just say we have it on good authority that Aurora may be held there."

"What authority are you talking about, folks?"

"Right now, Detective, let's just call it woman's intuition," Caroline deflects. "Besides, what other leads do we have?"

Fifteen minutes later Buster Bodine meets them at the entrance with a map of the area, and they discuss a plan.

"You realize, of course, that we're pretty much flying by the seat of our pants," Bodine states. "And you say we're maybe looking for an old religious alcove or something?"

"Yes," Delano replies. "A place that was here before it became a limestone quarry. It must be a remote space since we don't recall ever seeing it during our hikes. There is an ancient-looking nook carved out of solid rock, but we've never ventured near it. That's a possibility, but other than that, we should look inside several of the mining sheds."

Bodine rolls his eyes thinking this is a futile exercise, but he goes along with it.

Chapter 19

Heather Bee awakens stiff as a board after sleeping on the old, worn cot in the secluded reflection center. She looks over at Aurora and sees that she's still asleep on the other cot. She goes outside to relieve herself and collects some drinking water from the little brook in cups she bought at the grocery.

"Good morning, little one, it's time to wake up." Heather sniffs the air, and asks, "Does someone need a diaper change?" She gently lifts Aurora and takes her outside and bathes her in the stream. The water is chilly and the child squirms and cries until Heather dries her off and hugs her.

"There, there. That's better, isn't it? When we're in Florida, we won't have to worry about being cold ever again. Now, let's get us something to eat, and then we'll just sneak away. You and me, how's that sound?"

After eating she gathers their belongings and loads Aurora and everything in the Nash. She opens the chest containing the ransom money and smiles at her good fortune. "Sorry, Ricey Poo," she says out loud. "It was fun while it lasted, but now I'm past it!" She climbs into the driver's seat and starts the engine. Aurora lies peacefully wrapped in a blanket on the seat beside her.

Meanwhile, at the quarry entrance Bodine radios his officers to make certain everyone's in position. "There're a lot of old access roads in and out of this place, so keep your eyes peeled. I seriously doubt that anyone will show up for work at this early hour, but just stay alert. The Engels and I are gonna start moving into the quarry. Remember, we're looking for a Nash automobile with a female driver. Let me know the moment you spot anyone and don't go shooting up the place. We're here to rescue a child."

Officers Edberg, Hazel, Tweedie, and Wurster acknowledge the detective's instructions. Caroline and Delano pace anxiously and then follow the detective into his car.

"Ready?" he asks them rhetorically and begins slowly driving forward.

"How well did you say you know the quarry?" Bodine asks.

"Fairly well," Caroline replies. "It's close to our house, and Delano and I have been hiking here occasionally ever since he returned from the war, but I can't say we know every inch of it. You might want to see if you can reach the plant manager for the quarry. He and his employees would know the area best."

Bodine radios his office and asks them to see if they can reach the quarry supervisor and get him out here.

"We can't wait for him, though," Delano says. "We can't risk Heather Bee slipping away." Bodine nods his head in agreement and continues to pull his car forward slowly.

The morning sun has risen to the point where it's not necessary for Heather to use her headlights. Nonetheless the terrain inside the quarry is alternately littered with rocks and pocked with potholes. "Last thing we need now, sweetie, is a flat tire. That would really mess with our getting out of here, and I want us to do that before the quarrymen show up for work." She continues driving along dodging obstacles and gets very close to where she originally entered the quarry. She stops and rolls down her window to listen.

"I thought so," she whispers to herself. "I thought I heard a car up ahead and men's voices." She estimates that they're about a hundred feet away and haven't heard her Nash. Heather puts the car in reverse and makes a wide arc in an effort to turn around and go another direction. She nearly backs into a swampy area but manages to avoid it at the last moment.

"Jeepers, that was close!" She continues driving as stealthily as she can and comes to another possible exit. She slows to a stop and listens some more. Nothing. She waits a few moments longer, then continues slowly driving forward. From the corner of her eye she sees movement about a hundred yards away and tries to hide her vehicle behind a large rock. It's too late. She's been spotted by Detective Bodine.

"I think that's her!" Bodine shouts, and he and the Engels start driving toward Heather's position, but their path is blocked by a quarry vehicle. Bodine radios Officers Tweedie and Wurster. "I think we've found them, and they're heading your way."

The officers acknowledge and Wurster says, "Got 'em. She's coming up on us fast. We're closing the wooden gate across the road."

Heather yells, "Hang onto your diaper, Aurora, it's gonna get pretty bumpy!"

The officers stand in front of the gate and holler for her to stop, but Heather is having none of it. She guns the engine and drives straight at them. They dive for cover and Heather bashes her car right through the wooden gate and careens roughly off the front of the officers' vehicle. "That'll slow 'em down!" she shouts victoriously as she exits the quarry and fishtails onto Manhattan Road. A minute later Detective Bodine and the Engels arrive at the busted gate and stop briefly to see if his officers need medical help.

"She went that way," Officer Wurster points. "Back toward town."

At this time of day traffic is light, and Bodine stomps on the accelerator. He radios for assistance and gives the dispatcher the description of the Nash. The dispatcher puts out an all points bulletin.

Delano and Caroline are flooded with adrenaline, and he recalls what the Tamberg book had said to them earlier this morning…"Take Flight!"

Delano grabs the radio and immediately tries to reach Brian at the airport. "Brian, pick up! It's Del, We're heading your way. Need to have the Jenny fully fueled ASAP and ready for takeoff. Also, I want you to load a few of those special items we've been working on for the government. Put them in my cockpit."

A few seconds later Delano hears Brian's voice, "Copy that, Del. She'll be ready, including the things you requested."

Bodine speeds through town and east toward the airport. "What do you think, Detective?" Caroline asks. "Do you think Heather Bee will try to hide again somewhere?"

"I doubt it. My guess is she's gonna make a run for it. Try to get out of Putnam County and get lost in the countryside, or maybe try to get to Indianapolis and hide in a larger population."

"My hunch would be the latter, Bodine," Delano surmises. "Too easy to spot a single vehicle on a country road, but it's definitely a crap shoot. Drop us off at the airport, and Caroline and I'll take the Jenny up. We can stay in touch by radio."

Bodine races into the airfield, drops the Engels off quickly, then departs alone.

"No time to chat, Brian," Delano hollers over the sound of the engine which Brian had turned on for them. Caroline plops in her cockpit a moment after Delano does, and Brian removes the wooden blocks holding the aeroplane's tires. They're airborne in a matter of seconds and wave to Bodine as they sail over his car.

"Now where?!" Bodine mutters to himself. He does the only thing he can think of and tries to head in the same direction of the plane.

Delano gains altitude so he can have a broader view of the countryside. He flies the Jenny in wide circles hoping to spot the Nash's unusual body lines. The good news is that the sun is fully up and provides a well-lit view for him. The bad news is that there's a little more traffic this time of morning.

"Keep your eyes peeled, honey," he shouts to Caroline over the sound of the engine. "You know what her car looks like."

They fly for five minutes which feels like an eternity. They first head due east thinking that maybe Heather will try to drive to Indianapolis. They see nothing other than a few horse-drawn buggies and wagons. Delano then changes his heading in a northwesterly direction and lowers his altitude for a better view. It's everything that Bodine can do to try and keep up with him.

Delano radios Bodine. "You might want to hang back a minute instead of trying to keep up with us. I'm heading for the creek and will swing back if we don't see her car."

"Roger that!" Bodine responds.

They fly over Crow's bridge spanning Big Walnut Creek. It seems like a lifetime ago now that Delano had thought he'd found Aurora in the carpetbag under the bridge only to have a big tabby cat jump out instead.

Caroline and Delano are beginning to feel very anxious that they're not seeing anything promising. Then, Caroline shouts, "There, Del, I think that's her car."

Delano banks the aeroplane sharply and descends for a closer look. "Bodine, we're over Round Barn Road near the railroad tracks. We think we have a visual and are going down for a closer look. Suggest you meet us around there and call for backup."

The detective acknowledges Delano's sighting and does as he suggests. "Heading your way now! My officers should be arriving soon."

From the road Heather looks up into the sky and feels the warm sun on her face. She glances over at

Aurora who's playing with her toes and giggling. Heather sees a few turkey buzzards doing lazy circles as they ride the warm updrafts, and she thinks what a lovely last day it is in Greencastle, Indiana.

Then, she spots the aeroplane and begins to wonder if she's being tailed. "Uh oh, I think we may have unwanted company, sweet girl. Gotta ditch 'em fast." She cruises along and sees the big round barn the road is named for. In the blink of an eye she makes a quick left turn off the road and lowers her speed as she drives into the open barn to hide.

"Where the heck did they go, Del?" Caroline shouts. "We had her a minute ago, and now she's gone! Damn!"

Delano scans the area and sees that there are very few places for her to hide. "Hang tight, Caroline, I'm going in for a closer look." He brings the Jenny around and lowers his altitude to about fifty feet and flies directly at the barn. Closer and closer he flies, and just before he pulls up Caroline hollers, "The car's inside the round barn. She's hiding in there."

Heather knows that she's been spotted, and that it's got to be the cops. "Can't stay inside here much longer or I'll be trapped," she's says out loud to herself.

Delano quickly radios Bodine and tells him she's inside the round barn. He accelerates even more. Then, Delano tells Caroline to take over the controls and fly low toward the entrance of the barn. "I've got a surprise for Miss Bee."

Caroline isn't sure what her husband is talking about, but she does as he asks. Delano reaches down by his feet and lifts an aerial bomb that his family's company has been testing for the government.

"A little lower," he shouts to Caroline as they approach the entrance, and then he drops the aerial bomb which explodes about ten feet in front of the main entrance. Soil flies in all directions creating an impassable three-foot crater. Caroline screams, "Woohoo!" and Delano shouts, "Same thing, darlin', but on the barn's rear entrance this time!"

Just as Heather is about to make a run for it, she sees the areoplane low in the air coming at her position like an angry eagle, and then Delano drops another bomb near the rear entrance creating another impassable crater.

"Take us down now, Caroline, in that fallow field by the barn. Try to get as close as you can without wrecking the Jenny." Then, Delano radios Bodine. "We've got her trapped inside the round barn, Detective, and we're putting the plane down in the adjacent field. Meet us there!"

A minute later Caroline lands the Jenny just as Detective Bodine pulls up beside them. He pulls out his service revolver, and the three of them approach the barn.

"Give it up, Miss Bee, you can't escape, and we have more officers on the way."

Heather appears at the entrance to the barn. She's crestfallen that her dream of escaping to Florida with little Aurora is coming to an end.

"But she's mine," she blubbers. "I'm her new mommy now, and we were gonna go away together and start a new life." She's shellshocked from the explosions and the unexpected defeat. "Mine," she blubbers again.

"Give her to me!" Caroline demands, and after a final look into the child's face, Heather reluctantly releases Aurora. Caroline gently hands their little girl to Delano and then fiercely punches Heather squarely in the face. "You thankless witch!" Then, she rejoins Delano and the baby, and they share a tearful but very happy reunion.

Bodine places the sobbing kidnapper in handcuffs and leads her away. Two other squad cars arrive, and Bodine instructs them to take her to the county jail.

The detective smiles as he looks at the craters the aerial bombs made at the front and rear entrances to the barn. "Looks to me like you two had things pretty much in hand. Remind me to never get on your wrong side."

"Thanks, Bodine. You and your men have been great. We'll be happy to give you a full report on our aerial grenades later, but right now would you mind driving us over to Doc Kissel's office? We want to make certain Aurora is okay, and then we really want to go home."

Chapter 20

THE NEXT MORNING SEES a spirit of joy at the Engel house unlike anything they've experienced since the day Aurora was born. At first light Caroline slips quietly into the nursery and feels an incredible sense of relief that her baby is there and soundly sleeping. Delano joins her and places his arms around his lovely wife. "We got her back," he whispers in her ear. "And we're never going to lose her again," she softly replies.

Delano goes downstairs to the kitchen to make coffee and a wholesome breakfast while Caroline sits in a comfy chair in the nursery holding Aurora and rocking back and forth with a nurturing rhythm with each breath she draws.

The telephone rings and Delano races to answer it so as not to disturb mother and child during their bonding time together.

"Good morning, Mr. Engel, just wanted to make certain that you and the missus are awake before stopping by to finish my police report. Can I take it that Dr. Kissel's examination of Aurora went well?"

"It did, Detective, thanks for asking. The doctor said she seems to be in very good health, maybe a little dehydrated, but otherwise no worse for the wear and tear."

"Well, that's certainly a relief, isn't it? I was wondering if you'd be up for my dropping by in about an hour or so. I want to bring you up-to-date on where we stand with Rice Foxx and Heather Bee, and I have a few questions I want to ask you and Mrs. Engel."

"That would be fine, Detective, we're not going anywhere today. Just want to stay home and be a family again."

They hang up, and Delano tells Caroline that Bodine will be coming by in a bit. While Delano washes the dishes and puts things away, Caroline feeds Aurora and gives her a warm soothing bath.

Shortly thereafter Delano hears tires crunching on the gravel driveway, and he goes outside to greet Bodine.

"It doesn't appear that you got much sleep last night, Detective. How about a cup of coffee and something to eat?"

"You're right. I was up last night squeezing Heather Bee and Rice Foxx's heads for details about the kidnapping. Needless to say neither of them is very happy with the other. Each one is insisting that kidnapping Aurora was the other's idea. Fact is, we caught them both committing a federal crime, and they'll likely be wearing stripes for many years to come. How're you two and the little one doing?"

"Like you, tired, but we feel like the weight of the world has been lifted off our shoulders. Can't thank you and your officers enough for being there for us."

"Just very happy that everything worked out the way that it did."

Delano pours Bodine another cup of coffee, and Caroline joins them cradling Aurora.

"There's the star of the show!" Bodine says as he beams at the child. Actually, I should call all three of you 'stars of the show' considering that we wouldn't have been successful without you."

"We got very lucky," Delano adds.

"And, speaking of luck, how was it that you two had an inkling that Heather Bee would be holed up in that old religious alcove in the limestone quarry?"

Caroline shoots Delano a quick, private glance. "It's hard to explain, Detective, I guess you could just call it a mother's intuition. Not sure how else to really explain it. I just had this sense that Aurora was nearby, somewhere in the quarry."

Bodine is more than a little skeptical, but chooses not to press the matter since they got the ransom money back and everything turned out positively.

"Well, that's a pretty darn strong sense you've got, Mrs. Engel. Remind me to take you with me the next time I go to the racetrack."

"Deal!" she replies.

"So, what's going on with those aerial bombs you tossed down near the round barn? For a minute there I thought that WWI had come to Putnam County."

"Yeah, I think I may have mentioned to you before that our family has factories that are under contract with the government to make military-grade munitions. That's in addition to our making clothing and parts for the aviation industry. I had a few grenades left over and asked Brian to put them in my cockpit. A Curtiss Jenny's really more of a training aeroplane, but she's obviously steady enough to use in combat situations too."

"I'd say so! The combination of Mrs. Engel flying and you dropping bombs, uh yeah, I'd say your skills should impress the government folks very much."

"We got lucky," Delano replies again. "No one got hurt."

"There is one issue, though," Bodine says wryly. "Ol' farmer Zeller wants to know who's gonna clean up those craters your aerial bombs made at the entrances to his round barn."

The Engels laugh. "Tell him I'll stop by to see him in a day or so. We'll make it right with him. What else do we need to go over, Detective?"

"That's pretty much it for now. Obviously, you'll both be called to testify. Justice has a way of moving slowly sometimes, but like I said, Foxx and Bee won't be seeing daylight for a long, long time."

They shake hands, and the three Engels smile as they watch Buster Bodine slowly drive away.

"All's well that ends well, to borrow a phrase," Caroline sighs as she leans against her husband's shoulder. They look around their yard. The gardens need weeding, and the lawn needs to be mowed. Curiously, the stone angel sculpture doesn't look nearly as sad.

Delano murmurs, "We have a great home, a lot of work, but a great home." Caroline smiles and nods. Their eyes eventually settle on the roof tower, and they ponder what to do next.

"So, what do you want to do now, Del?"

"Perhaps, we should pay a visit to our, uh, friendly book in the attic. At the very least we need to pay our respects and acknowledge that it did everything it said it would do for us."

"I agree, sweetheart, and I doubt the detective or anyone else would ever believe us if we shared the truth about the source of our...intuitions."

They return inside and go upstairs to the nursery. Caroline places Aurora in her crib and lowers the window blinds. She kisses her child sweetly on her cheek and promises that they'll return shortly.

———

Delano and Caroline climb the attic stairs and enter the cedar closet. It feels like ages ago that they first discovered the hidden room. They look at each other knowingly, and Caroline presses the knot on the cedar panel. She takes her husband's hand, and they step through the doorway together. A golden glow emanates from the rolltop desk and permeates the small room as they approach. The Tamberg book lies open before them.

"We've come to pay our respects," Delano says. "To thank you for your guidance."

The sentient book glows even brighter and its pages flutter.

Yes, I sense that your family
is as it should be.
That you are whole again.

"We are whole again, and we are grateful beyond words." Caroline agrees. She waits a moment and then says, "We know that you have written that you are the sum knowledge of the Tamberg Magical Dynasty, but where do we go from here knowing that we share a home with a large book that sees into another realm? We have so many questions to ask you."

Indeed, so many questions.
You are not the first to ask me this.
Christopher and Elizabeth Wright
asked the same question.
Yet, they have come to understand that
not all questions require answers.

"See!" Delano interjects. "That statement begs even more answers. What did happen to the Wrights?

"You write as if they're still alive…and where have their belongings gone with the exception of you and an old, well-traveled trunk?" The sentient tome glows even brighter as if amused by the Engels' frustration.

Ah, the Wrights!
They've enjoyed good lives…
then and now.
And yes, the trunk…and its bounty.
A gift to Elizabeth from so long ago.
A wondrous gift that needs
to be fully appreciated.

Caroline and Delano look at each other with confusion etched on their faces. "We don't understand what you mean." The book replies as if it cares little for their total comprehension.

Yes, so many questions, indeed!
It has been many years since
we've been united,

The trunk and me.
I traveled here inside the trunk.
Perhaps, you will reunite us.
Perhaps, your questions may be answered,
Or, perhaps they will forever be
A part of the mysteries of life.

"Okay, I think we've read enough nonsensical gibberish for now!" Delano declares with annoyance. "Do you ever give a clear answer?"

I have given you all that
you need to know...

Delano lifts the great book from its perch on the rolltop desk and says to Caroline. "Let's see if we can get to the bottom of these riddles once and for all. Please bring Aurora and meet me in the carriage house."

The book stops glowing and remains silent as they leave the hidden room.

Chapter 21

A FEW MINUTES LATER Caroline meets her husband in the carriage house and places Aurora in her play pen. Delano sets the book on a table next to the trunk that is covered in old European travel stickers. It begins to glow brightly again.

Delano addresses the Book of Tamberg, "A while ago you wrote to us that Caroline and I were 'chosen.' Can you at least tell us what that means?"

The book's blank pages flutter, then cease.

Yes, but that doesn't mean you
will fully understand.

"Try us!" Caroline parries with frustration equal to her husband's.

The knowledge of the Tamberg
Dynasty is rooted in the past.
For reasons that go beyond
my understanding,
The three of you, and even
your business endeavors,
represent the way of the future.
While the Tambergs relied
on conjuring magic,
The world has now become a
place of scientific inquiry.
The magical realm is the old way.

It is ancient and its powers
were held by only a few.
Now, the world has finally
become egalitarian.
The Great War that you
endured taught us that.
The time to permanently
change is long overdue,
And you have been chosen
to help lead the way.

"But, by whom?" Delano beseeches. The book remains silent.

"I don't think it can, or will, answer that, Del."

"Ah! The mysteries of life...
And, remember,
Res Non Semper Videntur
Things are not always as they seem...
Behold the trunk!

"What do you mean, 'Behold the trunk'? We've been living with it for months!" Delano states. Caroline kneels down on the floor and begins examining every inch of the wooden trunk's exterior very closely.

"Looks like it always has to me, Del. Take a look and see if you notice anything different." Delano kneels on the floor and examines it as closely as Caroline had. "I don't see anything peculiar. Let's look inside."

They open the lid to the old steamer trunk, and the book begins to glow even brighter. Delano peers at every aspect of the trunk and taps his fingers here and there.

"Look, Del, unless I'm mistaken, it appears that the bottom of the trunk looks higher on the inside than on the outside."

It suddenly dawns on them. "It has a false bottom!" they almost say in unison. Delano taps on the bottom which sounds a little hollow. He finds a screwdriver and begins carefully prying the slats of the wooden base free.

"Got it!" he declares. Caroline sees old soft cloths wrapped around a rectangular object. She lifts the contents out from its hiding place and lays it on a table. The couple stare at each other, and Caroline unwraps the cloths. A mesmerizing painting of a starry night beams back at them. In the corner is an inscription and a signature with a large capitalized V.

> *For Cousin Elizabeth with love from*
> *Vincent van Gogh.*

"Oh my God, Delano, do you have any idea what this is worth?"

The Engels examine the wonderful painting and can't believe their good fortune. "It's beyond glorious!" Delano praises.

They turn their stupefied gazes to the Tamberg book, and it glows brighter still, until a shimmering golden light fills the interior of the carriage house. As if in a dream, animated images of Christopher and Elizabeth Wright appear within the room. They're smiling and waving to them as if celebrating a long mystery that's finally been solved. Elizabeth blows them a kiss and then the Wrights' golden visages gradually dissolve and return to an unseen realm.

"But wait...." Caroline stammers! "Where?" Delano tries. They look at the great tome, and a prophetic script scrolls across the page before the Tamberg book disappears as well.

Until we meet again...

~ The End ~

About the Author
Stuart Fabe

STUART FABE IS a creative man. For many years he wore a suit and organized charitable fundraising campaigns for important organizations in Cincinnati, Ohio, like Children's Hospital, the Jewish Hospital, and the Cincinnati Zoo.

But, everything comes and goes, and in 2005 he decided it was time to focus on something even more personally fulfilling…creating!

Since leaving his former successful career behind, he's become a widely collected photographer, an illustrator, and a published storyteller. *The Write House* is Stuart's eighth novel.

He resides in the bucolic countryside near Greencastle, Indiana, with his lovely partner, Marla, and together they contribute to the community that they care about and the people that they love.

www.ingramcontent.com/pod-product-compliance
Lightning Source LLC
Chambersburg PA
CBHW070018120726
47909CB00003B/979